Gaps in Stone Walls

BY JOHN NEUFELD

Aladdin Paperbacks

*In memory of my mother,
who would, I think, have
been proud of this book.*

First Aladdin Paperbacks edition July 1998

Aladdin Paperbacks
An imprint of Simon & Schuster
Children's Publishing Division
1230 Avenue of the Americas
New York, NY 10020

Also available in an Atheneum Books for
Young Readers hardcover edition.
Book design by Lee Wade
The text of this book is set in Sabon.
Printed and bound in the United States of America
10 9 8 7 6 5 4 3 2 1

The Library of Congress has cataloged the
hardcover edition as follows:
Neufeld, John.
Gaps in stone walls / John Neufeld.—1st ed.
p. cm.
Summary: Twelve-year-old Merry Skiffe, who lives on
Martha's Vineyard in the 1880s, runs away from home because
she is suspected of having committed a murder.
ISBN 0-689-80102-5 (hc)
[1. Murder—Fiction. 2. Runaways—Fiction. 3. Deaf—Fiction.
4. Physically handicapped—Fiction.] I. Title
PZ7.N4425Gap   1996
[Fic]—dc20
95-24317

ISBN 0-689-81640-5 (Aladdin pbk.)

According to the research of Alexander Graham Bell, at the time of *Gaps in Stone Walls* one out of every five citizens in Chilmark was deaf and, in nearby Squibnocket, one out of every four.

I have taken for my characters the surnames of real citizenry of the time, appending my own selection of first names. To my amazement, some of these combinations actually belonged to living residents of Martha's Vineyard in 1880. Their use is purely coincidental, and in no way do I mean to imply a particular man or woman was either deaf or hearing. According to research done by others, there *is* no way of knowing.

Long before the time of this writing, deafness on Martha's Vineyard as an hereditary event had disappeared.

John Neufeld
January 31, 1995
Los Angeles

Legend

1. Ned Nickerson's Farm
2. Peter West's Farm
3. Chilmark P.O. & Store
4. Methodist-Episcopal Church
5. Fairgrounds (W. Tisbury)
6. Tilton Farm
7. Norton Farm
8. Skiffe Farm
9. Vincent Farm
10. Grist Mill

Narragansett Sound

Indian Hill

W. Tisbury

North Road

Tea Lane

Menemsha Harbor

Tiasquam River

Middle Road (5+ miles)

Gay Head

Chilmark

Menemsha Pond (Bight)

South Road

Tisbury Great Pond

Squibnocket Pond

Atlantic Ocean

Martha's Vineyard
1880

Vineyard Haven

Cottage City (Oak Bluffs)

Nantucket Sound

Edgartown

W. Tisbury Road (Takemmy Trail)

Chappaquiddick Island

Katama

Herring Creek

South Beach

Wasque Point

N

0   2   4 miles

one

Twelve-year-old Merry Skiffe ducked her head and ran hell-for-leather across the Tiltons' north pasture. Sodden gray clumps of sheep shouldered one another nervously as she sped by.

The surprise autumn squall that pushed up at her from the island's south shore forced her to run bent nearly double. Its rain pelted her head and her shoulders. She could feel it soaking her dress. The extra weight of heavy damp clothes slowed her flight and—to her own surprise—rankled. How could she be both in fear for her life and angry?

She dashed through the Massachusetts scrub pine. Oak trees, stunted by ocean salt, shielded the Tilton homestead from winter storms. Terrified, she ran for cover behind a copse of young red maples to catch her breath, peeking through too-thin branches. She saw no one at the farm or in its fields. She prayed no one saw her. She had to reach home. She had to hide.

The raindrops that continued to drive into her thin frame now mixed with, and disguised, Merry's tears.

If what her friend Simon Mayhew said was true, she, too, was a suspect. She could be put in jail—for years! for her whole life! She could be hanged!

But how could anyone have known there were moments when Merry really had wished Ned Nickerson dead?

She had seen no one else on the beach. She was almost certain that Mr. Nickerson himself had heard no one else about, otherwise he surely wouldn't have . . .

Merry shut her eyes quickly.

Old Ned Nickerson had deserved to die!

two

Edward Walton Nickerson had lived in a grand house at the top of Indian Hill. It wasn't his.

The house belonged to his brother, Captain Stephen Nickerson, lost at sea aboard his sloop, *Scudding Breeze*. The ship had gone down in a sudden storm as she was heading west northwest towards Martha's Vineyard, sailing home from a provisioning voyage along the Massachusetts and Maine coasts.

No one could imagine why the *Scudding Breeze* had been so far out to sea that she had had to turn into the wind to try to make port. She was not part of a fishing fleet, and yet she had headed towards the island from the direction of open water.

Normally ships that sailed coastal New England stayed in close to the shoreline. From the north, seafarers usually came round Cape Cod, down past Chatham and Dennis Port. Then they cut across Nantucket Sound to put in at either Edgartown or at Vineyard Haven, until four years earlier known as Holmes Hole. From the south ships sailed through Long Island Sound into Narragansett Bay.

The path of the *Scudding Breeze* was a mystery. The Atlantic could be treacherous at any time of the year. When Captain Nickerson and all hands went down a fierce winter storm had isolated every offshore island. The only reasonable explanation was that the ship must have been bullied out to sea by wild northeastern winds.

Almost a month later debris from the *Scudding Breeze* washed up on the sand between Wasque Point and Herring Creek on the south shore of the Vineyard. There hadn't been much. Bits of sailcloth, seven shoes, some shattered timbers, a logbook on which every page of writing had bled into the sea. Only an embossed *Scudding Breeze* on its cover, faintly legible for having been deeply tooled into its leather, remained to relay its owner's fate.

All this had happened in 1875. Merry had been seven then. She herself had not seen the wreckage. What she could remember of that time was that the eyes of people who spoke to one another about the disaster changed as they communicated. At one moment they would be wide with astonishment and shock; at the next, narrow with suspicion.

At Chilmark's general store, which also served as its post office, people would often gather at the end of their day's work. Sometimes Merry's father would bring her along, alone or with one of her brothers or sister, for what had become, over the years, an evening social gathering that matched the one held during the day as people stood chatting, waiting for their mail.

The child Merry would hide behind her father's tall frame. She would peek around his hip and watch attentively as arms and hands flew in all directions while people shared the latest news or a joke. She knew the laughter she saw was both loud and silent.

Sometimes Merry couldn't tell one from the other.

three

People in Chilmark, and in Tisbury next door, talked every day until his death about Ned Nickerson.

Some made fun of him. Some tried to be understanding. And some hated him.

The one thing everyone on the island agreed was that Ned Nickerson was good for nothing.

When he inherited the estate—the house and livestock, the acreage and pond, the carriages and the dozen pieces of property his brother the Captain had purchased with his profits from the sea—Ned Nickerson could have chosen one of two paths.

He might have become a generous member of his community. He might have donated money to the Methodist–Episcopal Church, which needed it. He might have allowed neighbors to farm more property than he, Ned, could do successfully on his own. At least he could have hired as hands some of the men whose livelihood offshore in dories was so dependent on weather and tides and the whims of bluefish, flounder and cod, and whose families needed to be fed and clothed no matter what.

None of this appealed to Ned.

What did take his fancy was living as though he were a country squire dropped onto the island from an English novel. He imported furniture from England via Boston and New Bedford. He installed in the great hall of the Captain's house a chandelier that held more than fifty candles. He employed young women—and this was often remarked, *young* women—who were made to wear black-and-white uniforms, long black skirts and tops, white aprons without bibs, and who spent hours each day dusting and polishing every trophy Ned installed.

But the silliest thing Ned Nickerson did, according to his neighbors, was to hire two down-and-outs, one as groom and the other as coachman, for his traps and carriages.

Hiring the needy wasn't what tickled people's fancies. Their attire did. For Ned Nickerson insisted that both men— the toothless, bent, gray Gerry Daggett, a poor cousin of prosperous merchants in Edgartown, and the teenaged Bernard Cleland who more than anything else simply needed to bathe—had to wear what he called livery.

The Nickerson livery was designed and sewn to mimic that of a landed English lord: black shiny boots, vests in warm weather or cold, kidskin gloves and top hats, and, for Gerry Daggett, a knee-length driving coat.

Most people took the sight of these two weak souls, one atop the Nickerson carriage, the other hanging for dear life onto its rear, with good humor. Old Gerry and Bernard themselves seemed to understand and even share the snickers and smiles that followed in their wake. In Edgartown, on an errand for their master, they often allowed people to buy them a glass of cider or ale, sometimes even stronger spirits, and stood quietly as their generous hosts asked questions designed to provoke or tease.

Other people, those who lived up-island in Chilmark or on nearby Indian Hill in Tisbury, were less able to smile and allow that since Ned Nickerson had the money to do what he wanted, why shouldn't he make a fool of himself?

It was one thing for Ned Nickerson never to have lifted a finger in his life, to have fallen into a jam pot and more power to him. His royal ways could be tolerated, barely.

But it was something else again for Ned Nickerson to be greedy as Midas.

Through newspapers and penny-dreadfuls that were delivered by packet from the mainland, the farmers and families on the Vineyard had followed the stories and legends of bank robbers, Indians, settlers struggling across distant western plains before the Golden Spike had been driven. They knew and read about the hardships of pioneer families on the trails heading west through Nebraska and Colorado, fighting mountain storms and hungry cougars and rogue Indian chiefs. They knew about cattle-rustling.

Out West people might be called rustlers.

On the Vineyard, the word used was "thief."

four

The early October storm eased. Soaked head to toe, Merry looked across the Tilton pasture towards her own family farm. Beyond the fields, past the stone walls, above the horizon hanging over the sea was a rainbow.

She bent down, still hidden from sight by the ring of young trees in which she had sheltered. She unlaced her tall wet shoes and drew them off. Because damp leather thongs could dry hard and tight, she carefully knotted the laces and lifted them over her head and onto her shoulders. She could run faster barefoot, anyway.

She was about to stand when a shadow sped past her. Instinctively she stayed low and peered out through dripping branches. Simon!

He had run right by, careening like a wagon out of control.

Without even thinking, Merry sat back hard on the wet grass. She drew her knees up and put her arms around them; her head was low on her chest, her eyes squeezed tightly shut.

Now what? Simon would tell her mother. Simon would probably tell everyone he met that he had heard the constable from Edgartown call out the names of four people who had no alibis for the night Ned Nickerson was killed.

What could she do? What was she supposed to do?

Merry lifted her head suddenly. There was only one thing she could do, she decided. She would have to run away.

Tears came into her blue eyes. She didn't want to run away. If she were honest, she would admit that sometimes she felt frightened when she wasn't at home on the island.

But she couldn't be timid now. She would have to be brave. At least, though she hadn't cottoned to each experience, she had travelled.

Once her father had taken all four of his children to Cottage City to ride the railroad back down to Edgartown. He had bought tickets for them all and put the two girls and Pickup in the charge of Ezra, his older son. As they climbed the thin tin steps into the railroad coach, their father had waved encouragingly at them before turning his trap around and starting out for Edgartown before the train.

And she had taken two other train rides since then, on real trains and over long distances, from New Bedford to Hartford, and back again. All alone, besides.

She had sailed across the Sound.

Merry sighed. She would repeat in her mind these victories. It was all right to be nervous. And certainly sensible to be cautious. But she *could* go away and survive. If she had to.

five

Merry picked her way home carefully and slowly. Knowing that Simon Mayhew was probably waiting for her somewhere along the north edge of her own farm made her both angry and amused.

Since the two had met at school as children, Simon had been convinced that Merry was fragile. That she needed extra care and comfort, extra time and patience. In a way, year by year Merry liked his attentions. But in another, they made her furious. She knew she was just as smart as he, and just as strong. It was only that she was a girl that put her in a special light in Simon's eyes.

Merry stayed close to the stone wall that separated the Tilton south pasture from her own north hillside. This wall ran south towards the shore; others led off from it to fence in and contain the Skiffe livestock.

There were cleared spaces wherever pasture allowed for the Skiffe gardens. Merry's mother, Molly, tended parcels of strawberries, apples and greens. Bailey Skiffe, Merry's older sister, tended the sheep and looked after the chickens. Pickup helped their father with the oxen and old Back-'n'-Fill, as well as with the old boar and two sows the Skiffes maintained for their offspring.

Merry stopped in her homeward progress at the edge of the family farm. She looked cautiously around a corner of her grandfather's house. She could see neither her grandmother nor any sign of Simon.

She paled suddenly. Of course there was no one about. Simon had given the alert and all had gathered at home to worry and decide what Merry should do.

What *was* she to do? She couldn't even begin to think about fleeing the island if she couldn't pack a few things to take with her. If Simon had alarmed her family, her entire plan would have to be changed. She would have to wait until the moment, probably at midnight, when she could slip into the woods that ran north along their property line towards the old Takemmy Trail between Edgartown and Tisbury.

Well, if she had to be brave, she might as well be clever, too.

She squared her shoulders and came out from behind the shingled corner of her grandfather's house. Within seconds, however, she was once again skittering along another stone wall. Brave was one thing; foolish another.

She halted her homeward progress where the wall gave way to a gate. The split granite posts were vine-covered, and between them—as all over the island—was a heavy wooden gate that had to be pushed open and then closed securely after one had come through.

The hundreds of gates on farms across the island stood silently for two things: protection of livestock, and a native—some said natural—desire to be left alone. Their great number made travel from one part of the island, from one township to the other, tedious work.

As she turned to close her own northern gate behind her and start towards home, Simon Mayhew stepped out to face her. Despite herself, Merry jumped back, startled.

" ~ Surprised you, didn't I? ~ " Simon grinned, kneeling then before her, reaching out with both hands to grab the bottom of Merry's dress. He twisted the long cotton skirt and wrung out a lot of water. He stood up and looked at her expectantly.

~ What? ~ Merry asked.

Simon shrugged. " ~ You ran away so fast, I was worried about you. ~ "

~ No need. ~ Merry was terse.

" ~ It's not so bad, you know, ~ " Simon told her. " ~ I have a plan. ~ "

~ A plan for what? ~

" ~ To prove your innocence, ~ " Simon said confidently. Merry widened her eyes. " ~ A girl like you couldn't possibly have killed Ned Nickerson. You're not strong enough. ~ "

~ Maybe I am. ~ Despite her frantic fear, Merry couldn't help but be annoyed by Simon's attitude. ~ You don't know everything. ~

" ~ I know enough, ~ " Simon argued.

~ You're no taller than me, ~ Merry pointed out. ~ Bet you don't weigh much more, either. ~

" ~ I do so. And I run faster. ~ "

Merry closed her eyes as she shook her head, her curls still damp from the rain. ~ What is this plan of yours? I need to know, now, because I've got one of my own. ~

" ~ You do? What is it? ~ "

~ Never you mind. If I told you, it wouldn't be secret anymore and you'd probably want to join up. ~

" ~ You're talking pretty sassy for someone who's in trouble. ~ "

Merry shrugged, but inwardly she thought Simon was right. She still couldn't imagine who had raised the alarm, who might have mentioned that late afternoon on the beach to the constable.

" ~ Here's what I think, ~ " Simon said after a second. " ~ As far as we know, there're only four of you who can't be accounted for. We have two choices. We can try to find someone who saw you in the fields, or we can find someone else to swear that Mr. West was not at home and old Gerry Daggett wasn't where *he* said he was, either. ~ "

~ You mean drunk at the bottom of Tea Lane? ~

Simon nodded. " ~ Exactly. ~ "

~ And what about Henrietta Chapell? ~

Simon frowned. " ~ Who knows? She was at Nickerson's house for nearly a year before being dismissed. ~ "

~ You tell my folks? ~

" ~ About what? ~ "

Merry drew a circle in the air with her right hand and arm. ~ Everything. ~

" ~ You don't think much of me, I guess, ~ " Simon decided. " ~ I wouldn't do that. I just went to see if you were home. I didn't say a word more. ~ "

~ So? ~

At first Simon was puzzled. Then he understood. " ~ So, first we have to trace your steps. From the store to here. Your exact steps. ~ "

~ Why? ~

Simon sighed and spoke slowly, patiently, as though to a child. Whenever he did this, Merry wanted to hit him. " ~ Because then we'll know where you went and where you were close to. If we know that, we have a chance of finding someone who looked out a window, say, or maybe heard you on the road. They might have forgotten about it, you see, it not being very important at the time. ~ "

13

There was too much unease in Merry's mind to allow hope to be kindled. Her features darkened. ~ When? ~

" ~ Why not start now? ~ "

Merry shook her head. ~ Too many people heading up to the store, ~ she explained.

" ~ So what? ~ "

~ They'll see us. Me. I don't want people to see me. ~

" ~ You can't hide, Merry. Besides, everybody up-island knows you, what you look like. They're your friends. ~ "

Merry's backbone straightened. ~ Tomorrow. Early. First thing. ~

Simon looked doubtful but said nothing.

~ Six, ~ Merry decided. ~ Before school. ~

" ~ Meet you right here? ~ "

Merry nodded.

So did Simon.

After a moment, Merry slipped past her friend and continued down the slope towards her own farmhouse.

She would give Simon a chance. At least for one day. After that, well . . . she would have to make her own choices, frightening though they might be.

As she walked she thought again about Ned Nickerson. Until that stormy afternoon along the ocean, she had only seen him crossing the island from time to time, or stopping at a wall to sit atop his Irish hunter seeming to dream, gazing at the field of cattle or sheep before him.

He seemed no older than her own father. In his saddle, on his gigantic steed, though, he looked twelve feet tall. He wore expensive clothing and his boots were shined brightly enough to reflect even a pale sky.

Merry could not recall his ever greeting anyone on a path or in church, and of course he never came to the store to shop or to collect mail. He had other people to do that for him.

From a distance, he didn't *look* frightening or mean or dishonest. But up close, that late spring afternoon, he had seemed huge and terrifying. No matter his words, his eyes had seemed demonic.

Merry tried and failed to push the past aside.

There were many tales about Ned Nickerson, about his habits and the way he showed off everything he owned. Showed off things he didn't really own. Perhaps even her own father's merino ram, gone missing since Sunday week.

Merry would have bet a penny the ram was at that moment captive in one of Nickerson's hilltop pens, his clipped right ear probably still scabbed from having been second-notched to disguise him.

Ned Nickerson deserved no pity.

six

Bailey Skiffe was one of the island's great beauties. Four years older than Merry, and only one behind Ezra, she was taller than her brother had been, but also, befitting a young woman, narrower and more graceful. Her long blonde hair was usually wound around the back of her head in a bun, and during springtime Bailey liked to weave wildflowers into it each morning.

Bailey was a hard worker. She never grumbled at her father when, because Pickup was missing in the neighborhood once again, she had to take up her younger brother's chores. And she never scolded Pickup, either, when often past dinner he would reappear scraped and muddy, wearing a shameless grin that spread even up and across the top of his tiny nose. He knew he was the family favorite. He could get away with anything.

More often than not Bailey would greet her little brother with a laugh and a light tap across his backside, and then sit down immediately to hear about his adventures. She listened with wide sparkling eyes, laughing to remember the things she herself had done at his age. And when Molly Skiffe's patience wore out, and she demanded that Pickup take to his bed without eating, nine times out of ten it was Bailey who quietly selected a cut of spring lamb or an ear of steamed corn or just a piece of bread-and-jam to take upstairs with her later to pass along to Pickup.

The tenth time, out of ten, Merry herself would do the same.

It had been the birth of Pickup six years before that brought renewed and carefree laughter and joy into the Skiffe house. He had been christened "Thankful" just four days after his birth.

"Thankful" was a Puritan name, and usually given to girls. But the Skiffes felt themselves so blessed to be given a child with ten perfect fingers and toes, whose eyes right away followed sound, who seemed so sweet natured, that they stuck with the name that bespoke their happiness.

As the baby, as the favorite, Thankful understood early on how much he could get away with and why. By the time he was two and a half, he was such a terror, leaving trails of clothes and broken pots and muddied footprints on the clean kitchen floor, that his parents began to wonder if perhaps another name might have been better chosen.

At four, it was clear Thankful was going to do what he wanted, when he wanted, and how. And the what/when/how soon crystallized into being the sloppiest little boy in Chilmark.

From Thankful's point of view, why should he bother to be neat and courteous if everyone who followed him thought him cute and funny, even as they bent and crawled beneath furniture to collect toys and clothes and books that belonged to him?

"Pickup" just came naturally after that. It was the word

most often addressed to him. His family never even had to discuss this. Ever afterwards, Pickup Skiffe was his name.

Merry tiptoed into the house. She peeked around the great fireplace, her hand ready to grasp the banister that helped one climb to the loft upstairs. Bailey stood at the large family table, washing fruit. From where Merry stood, she could see Bailey's cheeks rounded, which meant she was probably whistling softly to herself.

Opposite Bailey sat Grandmother Skiffe, her gray head bent towards the full-length white apron she wore over her black dress, both her hands wrapped in cotton as she cleaned and polished the chimneys that belonged to the family's kerosene lamps. This was a task she hated, often complaining that using candles was not only cheaper but cleaner. She had no kerosene in her own house.

Merry took a breath and started to climb the stairs towards the sleeping-loft. She was half afraid she would find Pickup there, either napping or snooping. But the large room above the parlor and kitchen below was unoccupied.

She went quickly towards her small bed. She bent down to reach below it and pulled forth a suitcase in which she kept her private and secret possessions—although little in the house was private or personal with Pickup around.

She lifted the suitcase to her bed, careful not to scrape it along the floor. She snapped its single lock and opened it. There, below her sewing kit and her collection of pressed flowers, was the book her father had given her Christmas last. It was hand-bound and full of empty pages, big ones.

In a box at the bottom of her suitcase were her pens and colored chalk. A bottle of navy blue ink, some fine fur brushes, and a small palette for watercolors waited patiently below clean cotton rags.

She sat back on her heels, the book before her on the bed

surface. She began to page through her work. Leaf after leaf held careful drawings, some colored, most in pen and ink only, of her favorite things on the island: flowering beach plum, seaside goldenrod, shiny sumac leaves, hawthorn. Climbing roses snaked from the bottom of a page to its top, and sketches of arrowwood, blueberries, and pitch pine trees followed. There were matching scenes of rocks at Squibnocket Beach, the ocean moonlit on the right, shimmering at high noon to the left.

On other pages, farther back in the book, were her attempts to sketch wildlife, a more difficult task. Here there was a curious baby red fox; there were the soulful eyes of a fawn; the Skiffe span of oxen stood patiently beneath their yoke in the shade of red swamp maple under a cooling summer sky.

Merry turned to a fresh, unspotted page. With a frown of concentration furrowing her wide forehead, she smoothed the page and then held the book open while she uncapped her ink. Delicately she lifted a fine-pointed pen and dipped it into the dark blue fluid. She closed her eyes a moment and then leaned up against the bed on her knees and began to write.

Monday, October 4, 1880

This is what I know.
Saturday night last Mr Edward Nickerson was murdered. He was found lying covered by leaves at the bottom of one of Mr Hiram Vincent's walls. His horse was not by his side and at first the man who found him (Mr Jedediah Pease) thought Mr Nickerson had been knocked from his saddle as he tried to leap the wall on his horse. Some people think that Mr Nickerson had been riding back to Indian Hill from Edgartown where he might have had several ales or brandies in a public house. Others disagree,

saying that he would have cut cross country on his way from Edgartown, and that he was coming up from the South Shore instead when he was slain. My friend Simon Mayhew told me this today after school.

That Saturday night my father wanted to walk to the store. My mother could not for her duties in the kitchen and so he asked me if I would like to go with him and I said yes I would. Together we walked up through the Tilton place and cut cross Norton's and came to the post office where there were maybe eight or ten other people standing around and talking and telling each other jokes and then after a while I wanted to leave since I was the only child there.

It was growing dark. There was some traffic on the roadway since it was a Saturday and neighbors often call upon one another. There was a little moonlight but for safety's sake I stepped off the roadway and onto a path that ran not too far distant from it when I saw a sad little chewink flapping and trying to fly so I began to follow it in order to pick him up and see what was wrong and maybe bring him home to rest and heal.

After I don't know how long he slowed enough for me to swoop down and pick him up comforting and clicking to him all the while so very carefully I held him and began to start home again when a great horse flashed by in the shadows on the roadway which startled me so that I tripped in the dark and opened my hands and the bird fell to the ground. I was heartsick for he was flapping as he fell but he fell straight down to earth and landed so terribly hard but he was strong enough to start running from me again so I followed still thinking to save him although in the darkness he must have heard some sudden commotion nearby that caused him despite his exhaustion to duck and dodge and to disappear amid the ferns and roots beneath the trees so I lost sight of him which made me very sad.

Time was passing and even though I searched and searched for the little bird I was getting hungry too so after a while I continued towards home through the Tiltons' farm and then south along the path that divides their place from the Manter farm.

I met no one on the path or in the woods and I believe no one saw me until I came home and Mother told me she was worried that something might have happened to me and Pickup (rightful name Thankful) said it would serve me right and Bailey knuckled his head.

My father returned from the store later when it was beginning to get foggy because Pickup paraded around and then stopped to blow out his cheeks and swing his right arm around in a circle from his shoulder which is his way of imitating a foghorn and a lighthouse.

This is what I did yesterday, the Sunday following. I arose early and went out in the mist to sketch the stand of white pine that lies not more than a quarter mile from our front gate. I went to church and had dinner at home with my family. In the afternoon my sister Bailey and I went to the South Shore to collect saltmarsh hay and then we traded some of it for oysters with Jared Snipes (an Indian). Simon Mayhew came to visit and stayed until my brother Pickup swung a chair at him and hit him on his leg then my mother punished Pickup and made him clean out the chicken run. That is what happened to me.

Today Simon told me that Mr Nickerson had a wound on the back of his head which could have come from falling off his horse except no one believed that because Mr Nickerson was an excellent rider and had never been known ever to have fallen from a horse even during the recent war and because no one could tell whether he had truly been trying to jump the wall in the moonlight which no one believes or whether he had been riding along when someone who didn't like him stole up behind him and did him in and there are a lot of people in Chilmark who don't like Mr Nickerson because he is mean and greedy and steals other people's belongings mostly from the pounds around the island but no one really knows how he does it because there are never any witnesses in fact my own dear father's prize merino ram was found in the pound along the South Road Saturday night a week ago someone had led him there after he had broken through his fencing and come to tell my father who was going to go the very next morning to get him and bring him back home but by the time Father got to the pound there was no ram there only one of Mr Pease's calves which was sick and thin poor thing and no one wanted to claim her or even to feed her any longer so that she was given up for lost and no one paid any attention.

A sheriff's constable has come to Chilmark although I have seen him not. He arrived yesterday and came to our house while Bailey and I were on the strand. His job is to ask questions of everyone and then to try to guess who killed Mr Nickerson so he goes around and knocks on every door and speaks to every one he meets and writes things down and nods and then goes away again to ask other people what they know or saw or heard on that dreadful night and when he decides who the guilty person is he will take him with him back to Edgartown to trial there and to prison and maybe even to his death.

So in the matter of Mr Nickerson's death no one saw me Saturday night until I came home from chasing the damaged bird and it was dark then and I forgot I did go out again that night to the privy when it was very black and thick with fog but I came in right away and went to sleep even though Pickup had folded my sheet back and I nearly tore it putting my feet beneath my covers.

That is what I know.

seven

Merry closed her notebook carefully after smoothing its pages. Footsteps on the wooden stair behind her did not resound in her ears. A single penny tossed onto the coverlet of her bed, however, caused her to look quickly over her shoulder.

Her father walked to where Merry was still kneeling and looked down at her, a sympathetic smile on his lips. Suddenly Merry began to weep, her shoulders shuddering up and down, her stomach aching. She reached out to touch her father's leg but even as she did she was lifted from the floor and held against his body, being rocked lovingly.

Her father stroked her hair and held her fast. For a time Merry embraced his waist, comforted by the smell of his muslin shirt, the feel of his braces. After a few moments, Merry's thin body edged slightly away as she controlled her sobs. She looked up into her father's deep brown eyes. ~ I didn't do anything! ~

Her father nodded. ~ I know that. We all do. Don't be frightened. ~

~ But the constable, the sheriff . . . Simon says only four people— ~

Benjamin Skiffe nodded. ~ He'll find out he's wrong about you. No one knows about Gerry Daggett. But Peter West is too good a farmer to worry about Ned Nickerson. Doesn't have the time. Henny Chapell did have the time, since being dismissed. I'm sure they'll all be questioned. ~

~ Questioned? ~ Merry's hands flew. ~ Where will I have to go? I'm frightened. Will other people—? ~

Her father untied his neckerchief, dabbing Merry's cheeks, and then stuffed it into the back pocket of his work trousers. ~ A lot of what the man has to do he just has to do, to satisfy other people, to please the sheriff. I'm sure he doesn't think you had anything to do with this. ~

~ But I have no proof! ~

~ Neither has the constable. Mr. Nickerson's death is a mystery, dear, and a mystery it will forever remain unless the sheriff's office finds out a lot more than it knows now. Calm yourself. Be honest as you've ever been and no harm will come to you. ~

Merry looked doubtfully at her father. ~ I did nothing more than anyone, ~ she complained. ~ I am often alone when I draw. And I can't be the only person on the island who walks freely about of an evening. ~

~ Of course you're not, ~ her father comforted. ~ Nor could you have known what was to occur Saturday last. We know that, Merry. Believe me, ~ he added. He reached out once more to bring his daughter into his arms and they stood that way, close and trusting for a moment when suddenly Pickup's freckled hand grabbed his father's arm.

Benjamin Skiffe turned his head and looked down at his son, not yet ready to release Merry.

" ~ Mama wants to know when you're coming down to tea, ~ " Pickup announced.

~ In a moment or two, ~ answered his father.

" ~ So, ~ " Pickup said, looking suspiciously past his sister at the suitcase on her bed, " ~ what are you two talking about? ~ "

~ Nothing that concerns you, son. ~

" ~ How do I know? Maybe it does. ~ "

~ It doesn't. Now, get back down those stairs and tell your mother we'll be along soon. ~

" ~ But what I want to know is— ~ "

~ What you'll find out is how the toe of my boot feels against your bottom if you don't move fast. ~

Pickup looked at his father and saw the smile that accompanied his warning. But Pickup was no fool. He never wanted to test his father into following through on any threat of punishment. He turned quickly and ducked down the wooden flight.

~ A group of us are going up to Nickerson's tomorrow at dawn, ~ Merry's father told her. ~ The constable is coming with us. We're going to look to see whether Ned Nickerson was the thief we think he was. I think it would be good for you to come along, too. ~

Merry's thoughts ran on two tracks. ~ What about school? ~ Then, immediately: ~ What could I do? ~

~ Nothing, just be with me. The more the constable sees of you, the less likely he is to be suspicious. Don't worry about school, dear heart. One day missed is no worse than a cold. Besides, Pickup may need some help. ~

~ Doing what? ~

Merry's father smiled. ~ If we're right and we find what we hope to there, we'll be leading our ram and two or three of his harem back down the hill towards home. ~

Merry thought this over. She had promised to meet Simon

25

at six so they could begin tracing her route and looking for witnesses.

She nodded that she would accompany her father. She stood a second on tiptoe and kissed his cheek. Then she slipped around him and started down the steps. Playfully he reached out as he followed her, pulling her nearly undone braid.

She would leave Simon a note in their secret place.

" ~ Well, at last, ~ " said her mother as the two reached the kitchen. " ~ Whatever was going on up there? ~ "

" ~ Merry was being given a talking-to, ~ " Pickup declared.

Merry ignored her brother as she went to help Bailey bring sandwiches and cakes to the table. In the corner near the bread oven sat her grandmother, her head low on her chest, snoring softly.

" ~ Merry, dear, ~ " said her mother, " ~ would you give us some light? ~ "

Merry nodded and went to the mantelpiece over the ovens. She reached up for one of the family's pewter candlesticks and, beside it, a pewter jug filled with strips of white paper tightly rolled: spills. Bending down gracefully, she put one of these near the coals of the bread oven and watched as the paper caught light.

She walked to the center table and applied its fire to the wick of the lamp there, holding in her other hand its flue. Careful of the flame, she settled the glass once more upon the copper base of the lamp.

She stood a moment, inhaling the scent of burning oil and wick. In her mind she was beginning to compose the message she would leave for Simon under the ledge.

eight

It was still dark and foggy when Merry slipped her note to Simon into their secret space—a sliver of a gap between boulders in the stone wall that separated the Skiffe property from the Tiltons'. She had not been able to think of anything more to say than what was true. "Can't go. Tomorrow instead. Same time."

She meant to turn then and run back home before anyone else was awake, or breakfast had begun. But the lightening of the sky in the east, barely strong enough to break through the mist and to begin to throw weak shadows across the woods and fields through which she would run, stopped her.

She stood a moment motionlessly, smiling. Indian summer was an unexpected gift, warm and scented, a surprise itself just as its startling storms and confusing winds folded and flew around one so suddenly.

Merry loved the island so much that she had begun to think of it as her own, her safe haven. Yet there were many places on it she had never explored. The cliffs at Gay Head and the tiny Indian village just to their south. Lambert's

Cove, which she had seen coming back from Hartford on the steamer, with its curling coast and sturdy hills above. Not to mention half of the freshwater ponds that ran along the South Shore all the way to Edgartown.

She began to amble through the underbrush in the general direction of home. Edgartown was so much different from Chilmark. It was flat, that was sure. Chilmark had hills and glens and cliffs and rocks offshore. Edgartown was just there, at sea level, a scant dozen miles away but really a whole world, she knew.

Edgartown people did different things and thought differently, too. They didn't think highly of "Up-islanders," which is what she and her family and all her friends were. They seemed to think they would as soon sail to China as cross the length of the Island to see its other end. And Merry knew enough of history to know that that was exactly what people in Edgartown had done for years—sailed off to discover farther shores and stranger people in whalers or clippers or trading vessels of seaworthy size.

What these voyages provided could be seen easily by anyone strolling through the streets of Edgartown: wealth. Merry's family—most of the people she knew in Tisbury and Chilmark—farmed and fished. Anything grown or caught that was more than an immediate need was stored or sold. Small boats would sail from Menemsha to New Bedford to trade, returning in a single day.

Edgartown boats sailed out to crisscross the seas, returning with silks and handpainted china and fine foods and spices. Its natives sold these to others in town, or in Boston and on the Cape. Money seemed to never stop sailing into port. Water merchants, like Captain Nickerson, built huge clapboard houses, framed by forest green or black shutters, that stood proudly on every small rise that gave onto the sea, their chimneys stretching into the sky above them.

Merry's own house, with its single chimney visible now just above the trees ahead of her, was not much different from her neighbor's: it, too, was wood but shingled and dark, stained against the weather. Its inside walls were wattled—daubed by hand to fill the spaces between timbers that separated its rooms—and then whitewashed. Downstairs was a parlor to one side of the central fireplace, and on the other side was a kitchen.

Behind these two rooms, added on at the back of the house, was a lean-to that ran across the width of the building. This was divided into three small spaces: a buttery for food storage, a borning room where she and her brothers and sister had first seen daylight, and a small bedroom for her parents.

In the loft upstairs were the beds and trunks for the Skiffe children, once four now three.

Merry pulled open her front door as slowly as she could. Even before she was inside the entry she smelled her mother's cranberry bread and knew she would have to explain her early-morning errand. She smiled to herself. She could say she was just in the privy but she knew that every morning, early, each family member repaired there first thing and if she had been there, door closed behind her, someone would have seen her emerge.

" ~ Merry, dear, where've you been? ~ " asked her mother.

Merry decided to tell half the truth. ~ Walking in the mist. I like it. ~

Molly Skiffe smiled. " ~ I bet if there were twenty-four hours of daylight, you'd be out sketching and walking, wouldn't you? ~ "

Merry nodded. ~ I imagine. ~

Her father appeared. ~ Ready? ~

" ~ You three can't go 'til you've eaten, ~ " Merry's

mother cautioned. " ~ Besides, I haven't finished putting up your meal. ~ "

Pickup clambered down the stairway from the loft. "Merry can get by on berries."

~ What? ~ Merry asked.

Pickup sighed. Every so often he forgot. A boy couldn't remember everything all the time, could he? " ~ I said, you'll only eat berries, anyway. We don't need a big meal. ~ "

" ~ Well, I like sending you all off ready for anything, ~ " his mother said. " ~ Besides, you and your father have enormous appetites. ~ "

Benjamin Skiffe smiled a little and winked at his wife. ~ True. ~

" ~ And take your oilskins, ~ " Molly advised. " ~ Unless I miss my guess, we'll have a downpour before the day is out. ~ "

The three Skiffes set off not long afterwards, Molly Skiffe's victuals wrapped in linen and paper, neatly arranged in a hamper with ham and chicken seated in separate packets at its bottom.

Pickup sat beside his father on the trap. Merry had asked that the rear seat be folded down so she could sit the way she preferred, dangling her legs over the back, watching the fog begin to lift above ground level, looking for her day's first glimpse of the sea above which they were rising.

The journey across the island to Indian Hill and to Mr. Nickerson's mansion there would take more than two hours. The distance wasn't great, perhaps just four miles. But Ben Skiffe's old sorrel horse, Back-'n'-Fill, made hard work out of everything he was asked to do.

As he grew older, Back-'n'-Fill was more and more testy. His mouth seemed to have grown harder, his teeth steel, and his temperament each year leaned more towards stubborn than not. Even Ezra hadn't been able to coax Back-'n'-Fill into obedience. It was Molly Skiffe's theory that the horse resented always doing the work that in richer families would have been done by two horses and sometimes by four.

Facing backwards, Merry forgot the alarm of the day before, rung by Simon, that she was a suspect in a murder.

A weak early-morning sun tried to warm the hillsides and the dirt path on which she rode, and the air became day-fragrant with the odors of herbs and cut grasses, and old Back-'n'-Fill. Only occasionally did a rock jolt the three Skiffes as it was crushed beneath their wheels.

Merry might have dozed but for the fact that suddenly she was aware of other people on the road, walking or riding in the same direction as she. The Luces came by, the entire family, nine of them, packed into their Spring wagon and waving gaily as they passed Back-'n'-Fill and his passengers. Merry saw old Grady Hillman walking alone, leaning on his cane, a small wire cage with two of his prize chickens in his other hand. He looked up and nodded at her.

Then, in quick succession, the Skiffes saw the Butlers, the Allens, the Manters. Greetings and smiles were exchanged between families and then their paths diverged, the Skiffes continuing along South Road where it turned north, leaving the other families to point towards the east on Middle Road and towards what Merry had also forgotten about: the annual three-day Martha's Vineyard Agricultural Society Fair.

Merry watched the backs of her neighbors as they made for the fairgrounds. Then she swung around to see Pickup jabbering at her father. She smiled to herself, knowing without being told what he was going on about. He wanted to spend every day at the fair.

Benjamin Skiffe, as long as his daughter could recall,

always went only once, on the fair's last day, Thursday. There was just too much work for the whole family to see to otherwise. He saved the fair as a treat, no matter how much Pickup pleaded and reasoned and begged.

Merry, too, had asked repeatedly to go every day when she was younger. Her father's response had always been the same. No matter what Merry said about her friends being able to go more than once so why couldn't she, Benjamin Skiffe shook his head. ~ I don't mind what the others are doing. *You* may not. ~ Pickup was probably getting that same message now.

Merry stopped smiling as Back-'n'-Fill drew even with the Spring wagon of her aunt and uncle, Elizabeth and Jeb Norton. With them, riding behind, their backs against the front seat and their long legs stretched out on the wooden flooring, were their three nearly grown sons, Merry's cousins: Sam, James, and Johnston. Eleanor, Merry's best friend, had been left at home.

Both families came to New Mill Brook, which had to be forded. Even though the creek's clear water was shallow, at this juncture in the road it was wide. No one wanted to damage a cart by riding across the water too quickly, perhaps shattering a wheel on a rock that had slowly rolled down the streambed to lie waiting patiently to cause havoc.

Her Uncle Jeb's wagon slowed and so did her father's. Without a word of instruction, the three Norton boys jumped down from the back of their wagon. Johnston raised a hand up to help his mother down from the bench seat even as his father alighted from the other side.

Pickup and Merry, too, got down from their perches, as Benjamin began to lead old Back-'n'-Fill through the rushing stream. A split and planed pine log, only half a foot above the level of the water, lay across the stream for people to use in crossing.

Back-'n'-Fill was at first hesitant but then, suddenly, he lunged into the water so fast he pulled Benjamin Skiffe with him.

Once across, and reboarded, the purpose of the day's outing returned to Merry's mind. Ned Nickerson had been a thief. Together, they were all on their way towards Indian Hill to see and to claim what Nickerson had stolen from them.

Ned Nickerson was dead. By whose hand, no one knew.

For a moment, Merry tried to shrink into herself, to get very small, invisible.

Questions were going to be asked, of her!

She knew, although she hated to admit this even to herself, that there *were* reasons a twelve-year-old girl might have to kill.

nine

Merry was on her knees, looking past the shoulders of her father and Pickup. Ahead, at the top of the final rise of Indian Hill, was the Nickerson house.

They had turned off the road and started towards the hill's peak, driving between the stone walls that bounded the Nickerson property from its neighbors. The walls were bare of moss or lichen. Being on a hilltop they were too often windblown and swept clean for anything to grow on them, even the tiny wildflowers that sometimes sprouted independently at lower elevations.

Merry's eyes were big with wonder. The house stood alone, more than thirty yards from any out-building. There was grass planted in a circle of gravel that was strewn before the main door. There were marble steps leading up to the entrance, and there were four tall windows on either side of the door.

The house itself seemed to stretch muscularly in the morning sun, its limbs longer and plain bigger than any

Merry had seen. At both ends there were additions made of brick, each with two chimneys. Merry was awestruck. What would it be like to live in such a house?

Before the Skiffe wagon reached the apex of the hill and was directed towards the right by a man dressed all in black whom Merry had never before seen, she caught sight of Gerry Daggett with Bernard Cleland hanging back behind him.

Gerry Daggett looked no worse than he ever did, Merry thought, except maybe for a slight tremble of nerves as he watched the Skiffes, Nortons, and a dozen other groups enter the drive and be directed where to stop their carriages. Merry wondered if she would be able to sneak off to ask Gerry what *he* thought of everything. To find out whether he was as afraid as she. Then, to her own surprise, she found she wanted desperately to go up and sniff Bernard Cleland to see whether he had bathed since his master's death.

The Skiffe cart halted beside that of the Nortons. Pickup and Merry jumped down from theirs as their uncle graciously handed his wife down to touch ground.

" ~ Well, Ben, what do we hope for here, eh? ~ " asked Mr. Norton.

~ One ram at least, ~ Merry's father replied. ~ With luck, three ewes that have gone missing since spring. ~

" ~ He was a canny man, that Ned Nickerson, ~ " Jeb Norton estimated. " ~ I don't doubt we'll all have to do a bit of squinting. ~ "

"I can recognize Woolrich in my sleep!" Pickup boasted.

"Bet he can recognize you, too," Johnston Norton laughed. "Just follow the path of a whirlwind."

Merry was standing rooted to the spot where she had landed as she got down from the trap. Her eyes were big as she saw for the second time, but really for the first important time, the man dressed all in black who stood in the center of the grass circle. He would have to be the constable, sent out from Edgartown. He would be the man sent to discover who had killed Ned Nickerson.

Merry was too young ever to have seen President Lincoln, alive or dead, but she had seen photographs in newspapers. Mr. Lincoln, in her mind, seemed serious but kind. This man seemed serious and serious.

She started as her father's hand landed on her shoulder and together they began to walk towards the grassy round. Merry tried to hide a bit behind her father's side but without success, for she saw the man in black see her and watched a look cross his features that she couldn't decode. Before she could think what next to do, she had been halted directly in front of him and pushed slightly ahead of her father. ~ This is my daughter, Merry. ~

"What?" said the man, confused by the language of Benjamin Skiffe's hands.

"This is my sister, Merry," Pickup explained. "My father said he told you about her before."

"Oh," said the man, "yes." He looked quickly to either side and then apparently decided to rely on Pickup. "Please remind your father that I come from Edgartown and am not well versed in his language."

"You aren't?" Pickup was astounded. With a broad sweep of both his short arms, he said, "*We* all are."

Merry watched and studied the man. He was tall and dark, with a thin beard that he had shaved from his upper lip but not his lower. His eyes were dark and difficult for her to fathom. He certainly did look serious.

"Will you ask your father what he hopes to find among Mr. Nickerson's herds?"

But before Pickup could finish his translation, Mr. Skiffe

was answering. ~ My merino ram and maybe two or three ewes. ~

Pickup told this to the constable who nodded and then, suddenly, turned away to speak to the crowd that had travelled up Indian Hill so early in the day. "Ladies and gentlemen," he began. Pickup stood seriously before his father, his hands poised, ready to go to work.

"My name is Franklin Fisher and I am deputy for the sheriff of Dukes County."

People nodded. Others watched Pickup first and then nodded.

"We are here today to examine the belongings of Edward Nickerson, recently deceased, against whom certain charges have been made posthumously."

Pickup worked hard but stumbled over that last word. It didn't matter, really, because Mr. Fisher's audience knew as much as they needed to.

Merry paid no attention to the announcements. Instead she stared at Mr. Fisher, trying to estimate whether he was married, if he had children, if he went to church.

With a start, she remembered that she was but one of four suspects. Gerry Daggett and Peter West, of course, but also Henrietta Chapell.

She quickly looked among her family's friends and neighbors. She wasn't at all certain what Henrietta Chapell looked like: apart from her service at Nickerson's, Merry knew almost nothing about her.

As for Peter West, absent, her father was probably right. Mr. West was a no-nonsense hard worker, whose farm was just off North Road, overlooking the tiny inlet at Menemsha. He was a deacon at church, and known to be stern but generous. To imagine him a murderer was more than Merry could do.

Suddenly she wished her cousin Eleanor were beside her so she could share her questions. Or at least Simon Mayhew.

"In an orderly fashion," Mr. Fisher directed, "let us go round the back to the stables and barns."

Pickup ran ahead of his sister and his father, and disappeared around the side of one of the brick additions to the mansion. Gerry Daggett and Bernard Cleland tried to hang back as best they could, but others behind pushed them forward.

The entire assembly moved down a small slope behind Nickerson's house towards sheds, barns, and pens. Merry was dazzled by the view—across the Sound all the way to the Elizabeth Islands.

Mr. Fisher held up his hand suddenly and the crowd halted its progress.

"I have had brought in every animal Mr. Nickerson was believed to own, rightfully or wrongfully. If—as you pass among them—you see an animal on which your sign is still in evidence, identify him and please bring him forward to be inscribed in the Dukes County tax census."

Pickup sent this message back fifty feet towards his father.

All was silent but for a few snorts or bays from the penned animals as the men from Chilmark and Tisbury carefully walked among them. Often a man would stop and reach out, sometimes bending down towards a sheep, sometimes reaching up towards a horse's head. Cattle could be examined easily, and goats more by their markings than by any branding or notched ear.

Pickup was jumping wildly among a small herd of merino sheep in a distant enclosure, waving his hand at his father. Ben Skiffe walked thoughtfully towards his son and reached out his right hand to touch the ram's ear. The Skiffe swallow-tailed notch there had been burned over, and Benjamin shook his head almost sadly to see the burn, which was still raw. On an island as small as Martha's Vineyard, and among friends, how could Nickerson have imagined people didn't know and recognize not just their own stock but that of their friends, as well?

That, after all, was what had given rise to the pounds situated across the countryside. Each pound was almost fifty feet square and built of the stones that came from the tilled fields nearby. They stood at least six feet high in order to harbor lost or stray animals until their owners could be sent for and come to collect them.

Self-enclosed and each with a gate that Merry thought resembled pictures she had seen of Stonehenge in England— the top crossbar usually being one long boulder balanced carefully atop two columns of split granite—the pounds were simply lost-and-founds for a particular neighborhood. Stealing from them, Merry thought, would have been like stealing money for the poor from the church box.

Merry stood apart from the busy crowd, wondering when or whether anyone would think that Gerry Daggett or Bernard Cleland were the henchmen who robbed the pounds for their master. Everything disappeared at nighttime, which made the likelihood of Gerry Daggett's being involved slim since he was known to like his drink. But Bernard?

She was startled from her reverie by feeling the dark eyes of Mr. Fisher fixed firmly on her from a distance of perhaps forty feet. She squared her shoulders and stared back at him, just the way she would whenever Simon treated her like a girl instead of a regular person. She didn't feel brave, but she knew she had to hold her head high no matter what.

Mr. Fisher broke his glance first, turning away just slightly to watch Merry's friends and neighbors approach him leading stock they could claim as their own. From his inside coat pocket, Mr. Fisher drew out a black notebook and a pen. He walked from one person to the next, entering in this book the animal claimed, the date best recalled as when it had gone missing, the sign or brand that bespoke chicanery.

Pickup had Woolrich by an ear and was pulling him towards the Skiffe trap. The Norton boys dragged and pushed two young Jersey heifers and an old cart-horse, good for nothing now but standing under a tree in the shade and remembering its own hardworking past. Other neighbors carried, pulled, or pushed piglets and boars, nanny goats and kids, spans of weary-looking oxen.

"Oh, I can tell you," said Merry's Aunt Elizabeth, "I'd love a peek into that house to see what else he's got. People say it's like a palace."

Her husband Jeb laughed and shook his head. "Not unless some of your own finery has gone missing, my dear. I imagine all that is going to Ned's sister, if ever she returns."

" ~ Will you be going to the funeral, uncle? ~ " asked Johnston Norton.

Ben Skiffe shook his head. ~ Can't grieve what you don't respect. ~

" ~ A good thing then old Ned never married, ~ " Uncle Jeb assessed. " ~ Would only hurt the feelings of his missus, then, wouldn't it, no one coming? ~ "

"Mr. Skiffe!"

Jeb Norton turned quickly around, seeing Mr. Fisher walking slowly towards the family group. He touched his brother-in-law's shoulder to direct Ben's eyes towards the figure in black.

"Would it be convenient for you to bring your daughter to the general store tomorrow at noon?" the constable inquired.

Jeb Norton passed the question on.

Benjamin Skiffe scowled briefly. ~ For what reason? ~

"I'll want to test an idea I have," explained Mr. Fisher via Jeb Norton again. "I'll want it to be witnessed by as many people as are interested."

~ What sort of test is this? I won't allow Merry to be hurt or frightened. ~

Mr. Fisher nodded his head in agreement. "Nothing of that sort, I assure you," he soothed. "Actually, I'll only want her, and a few others, to do one thing, to demonstrate for us all one thing. It won't take long and it's not dangerous."

~ You think my Merry is responsible for Ned's death? ~

Mr. Fisher actually smiled a little. "It's not easy to imagine, I know, and probably not. Still, just in case . . . I need to know a bit more about her than I do."

"Then you should just ask her questions," Elizabeth Norton said firmly, "rather than terrify the girl."

" ~ Merry's not frightened, are you, love? ~ " asked her uncle encouragingly.

Merry shook her head.

But she was.

Deathly afraid.

ten

Eleanor Norton was two years older than Merry and the only person Merry knew on Martha's Vineyard who understood *everything*, even if sometimes they disagreed. Merry was not at all certain Eleanor was as bright as other people said, but in a way it was nice to allow her to think she was.

Merry had ridden back from Ned Nickerson's farm with her cousins, squinched in between Sam and Johnston. James walked behind the wagon, leading one heifer and the spindly-legged cart-horse, trying like all get out to force the two animals to run uphill at a rise, then laughing when both refused to be grateful for their rescue or to think ahead to their welcoming mash when they were returned home. A second cow followed docilely the one James led.

The Norton farm touched one tiny corner of the Skiffes', nearer the sea and west out towards the cliffs of Gay Head. All of Merry's family surrounded her: the Nortons, at one edge, her grandmother on Ben Skiffe's property itself, and

Benjamin's two older brothers and *their* families each within a mile's walk.

It was only that her grandfather Skiffe, in a needy time after the War Between the States, had worried so about the future of his family that he had allowed the Tiltons to expand into his little corner of the island. Merry's father to this day said the economy, whatever that was, was still faltering. He liked the Tiltons well enough and they were good neighbors. He never faulted his father for selling.

Ben felt it was good to have something to rest on peaceably at bedtime. Apart from what produce and animals were sold through a season, this nest egg was all that stood between his family and charity. But the pillow old Mr. Skiffe's sale to the Tiltons provided wasn't all that comfortable when one considered it would have to be divided eventually into five parts, between his widow and his four children.

Eleanor herself, as the single girl in her family, was more spoiled than Merry. Also, she was schooled off-island. Every autumn she would sail across the Sound to New Bedford and take the train—the same one Merry had ridden but twice—to Hartford to attend the American Asylum for the Deaf and Dumb.

The state of Massachusetts paid Eleanor's tuition, and had done once for Merry, too, until Ezra had died and she had been summoned back to the Vineyard to help her family.

People on the island felt that children who went to Hartford returned better educated than those who took their schooling locally. It wasn't just that they had seen something of the world. They read better and faster, and they seemed to understand more fancy words than their companions in Tisbury or Chilmark. Often an adult, a grown person, would come to the home of a Hartford student to have read to him, or her, a difficult letter or a legal paper of some kind.

The only thing about her cousin that Merry found less than admirable was her vanity. Not that she was not pretty. She was. She had the same color hair Bailey Skiffe did, and was nearly as tall although she was two years younger.

What Merry disliked, just a little, were Eleanor's fancy manners. What people might call "airs." Merry thought them silly and she couldn't for the life of her understand why Eleanor behaved as she did: flirting with any boy she met, reaching out to touch the arms of grown men as she stood watching them talk, smiling eagerly when music rose at the fair and dancing was allowed.

Worse, from Merry's point of view, Eleanor danced well. Merry knew what envy was; she did not admire herself for her feelings, but she was jealous. She had never felt, nor sensed, the beats that Eleanor seemed so effortlessly to pick up and bend to. She had never understood what it was that she should feel through her limbs.

When the Norton wagon was in sight of their farmhouse, Merry looked up to see Eleanor standing at the doorway and waving to her. She waved back, glad once again she had come. She needed to talk to her cousin.

Jeb Norton helped his wife Elizabeth down while Sam eased the family bays from their traces and started to lead them away. James had gone round a corner immediately, driving his three charges to the barn. Johnston began to unload the wagon of its dinner leftovers and its jugs of pure water and early cider.

Merry jumped down into Eleanor's embrace.

~ I was so hoping to see you today, ~ Eleanor declared. Then, almost immediately, she put her arm over Merry's shoulders and her expression changed from one of greeting to one of dire concentration. ~ You poor thing! You must be terrified! ~

~ I don't know what to think, or what even to do first. ~

44

~ Well, I shouldn't wonder. What has got into those men, thinking you could even imagine doing anything like that? Not that someone shouldn't have, mind you. But certainly not you, dearest. ~

Eleanor began to walk with Merry to the back of the farmhouse towards a grape arbor set twenty yards from the kitchen. ~You wait here. I'll be right back. ~

Merry was plunked into a wooden chair, her cousin bustling away towards the house. Although a distant peal of thunder rang ominously in the distance, it was the darkening of the sky above that made Merry look up. Tall, full clouds were pressing down on the island from the northeast.

Within what seemed only a few seconds Eleanor reappeared, carrying a tray of cookies and lemonade. With a flourish that reminded Merry of her own mother, Eleanor laid the tray down and began unloading it, separating its glasses and plates, laying out serviettes.

When everything seemed suitable, or at least fit enough to please her, Eleanor herself sat beside Merry. Merry examined her cousin. ~ Are you feeling stronger? ~

Eleanor nodded. ~ Ever so much. ~

~ You've missed the start of school, ~ Merry said. ~ Are you sorry? ~

~ I'll be only a few weeks late. I shan't have missed much. ~ Suddenly and dramatically then Eleanor reached out for one of Merry's hands to hold in silence for a second. She shook her head sadly for just a fraction in time. ~ I've never forgotten what happened to you on the beach, you know, ~ Eleanor declared.

~ But you haven't told anyone? ~ Merry was alarmed.

~ Of course not. I am your friend. Your confidences are sacred to me. Still, what a horrible thing. What a horrible man. No one would blame you, you know, if . . . well, you know . . . ~

~ If I killed him? ~

~ Well, I certainly would have. Or at least would have wanted to. ~

Then, hardly seeming to draw another breath, Eleanor's face lit up and a huge smile crossed her even features. ~ Of course, you know I'm in love. ~

Merry was startled. ~ How would I—who? ~

~ Spaulding Mayhew! ~

Merry stared at her cousin. ~ Spaulding? ~

Proudly Eleanor nodded.

~ But he's— ~

~ One is allowed. It's simply a matter of fate whom one loves. ~

Merry understood. ~ But Spaulding doesn't do anything. I mean, he's barely Bailey's age. How could you—? ~

~ You forget, ~ Eleanor cautioned, ~ Spaulding's been away, like me. He's seen something of the world, even as a cabin boy. He has dreams, Merry. And they match mine! ~

~ But how would you both live? ~

Eleanor smiled wisely. ~ By our wits, dear. As the country folk say. ~ She clapped her hands. ~ I've already written to Marcella Ripon. You remember her. From our classes at school. She lives in Providence. That's where Spaulding and I will go first. Oh, it's going to be such a wonderful adventure! But you must never say you know! ~

~ Why? ~

~ We're going to run away! ~

Merry simply stared at Eleanor who nodded quickly. ~ On Thursday night, when the fair's ended. In all the confusion of packing up the competitions and displays, and when the dancing ends, we'll ride off to Vineyard Haven. We'll catch the first steamer the next morning and disappear! ~

Merry was dumbfounded.

Eleanor jumped up from her chair, taking two or three light little steps in a twirl before she stopped suddenly and looked more seriously at her cousin. ~ You know, you must believe me, that as soon as Spaulding and I are settled somewhere, that we'll . . . well . . . we'll think of you and invite you to visit. I mean, I guess that is, assuming that nothing— ~

Merry stood up too, quickly. ~ Eleanor, you think I did kill Ned Nickerson, don't you? ~

~ Of course not, dearest. But there's so much mystery, isn't there? Peter West is honest as the day is long, and respected. Poor Henrietta Chapell hasn't the wit. And I can hardly think that Gerry Daggett was ever sober enough a day in his life to have done anything like this. ~

~ So you've decided it has to be me? I'm to go to prison or maybe hang because you can't imagine Gerry Daggett sober, or Henny Chapell in a fury of some kind? ~

Eleanor frowned a bit. ~ Well, probably not just me. ~ She brightened. ~ But let's not think of that worrisome event. Congratulate me, dearest. I'm leaving with the most wonderful boy! ~

Merry had turned away and had begun to stride across the lawn just as the first few giant raindrops began to fall. Eleanor ran after her and caught her by her elbow. ~Promise me, now. You won't give us away. Promise! ~

Merry looked at her cousin with as much coolness as she could bring to the surface. How foolish she'd been, imagining that Eleanor would be sympathetic, would help her find a way to begin to solve her dilemma. How she wished she had never told her about Mr. Nickerson on the beach.

~ Promise, ~ Merry agreed.

Tearful, she turned once again to walk across the Nortons' east field towards her own homestead, putting her oilskin over her shoulders.

eleven

Merry strode through tall grass, her mind calming despite the roiling of the storm above. It was the Christian thing to do, after all. Realize others' problems and be sympathetic. That someone couldn't turn her cheek and do the same for you, well, that was something you just had to live with.

Merry suddenly felt herself shiver, and not because of the rain. Forget about Eleanor and Spaulding, she told herself. What mattered was that Eleanor imagined she was guilty of killing Ned Nickerson. If Eleanor did, others might, too.

She tried to remember everything she had seen and done that morning up at the Nickerson farm. She tried to recall whether she was the target of sharp or suspicious looks, whispered asides. Had someone treated her differently than before? Certainly not her aunt and uncle or her cousins.

Of course, Mr. Fisher would have been distant, but they had never before met and, given the circumstances, Merry could understand why he should be. She wondered whether her father's idea—putting them together so that Mr. Fisher would see immediately that Merry could not be the fugitive he was seeking—had worked. She doubted it. After all, she had to undergo *something*—she couldn't imagine what, exactly—in public the very next day at noon.

What kind of ordeal *was* she facing? Her mind raced. Would she be sworn and questioned in front of her family and neighbors? Was there something Mr. Fisher knew she had done that might throw more suspicion on herself? Had someone unknown seen her and Ned Nickerson on the south shore that day so long ago?

If Eleanor doubted her, pretty and bright as she was—although from Merry's point of view not thinking in a straight line about anything: Spaulding was the only object in her eyes that mattered—other people would, too. That was the really frightening thing. That meant that whatever she faced tomorrow, she wouldn't be innocent in some people's minds, no matter what she said or did.

Merry stopped in her tracks. She clenched her eyes shut. Her hands made fists and she beat them rhythmically against her thighs, feeling determined but also powerless. What was she to do?

She opened her eyes. Ahead of her, just coming across the field towards her, visible despite the rain that had grown torrential now, was Simon Mayhew.

Merry waved frantically and started to run towards him. There wasn't a moment to lose! She couldn't afford to wait until tomorrow at dawn to retrace her steps. They would have to begin tracking her route from the post office immediately.

If what Simon hoped for could be found—a witness, Merry needed that man, or woman, or child, at the post office tomorrow at noon. Desperately.

twelve

~ I can't remember *every* step! ~ Merry argued.

She was drenched and tired. A break in the storm had appeared but no warm wind arose to dry her dress or her boots. Simon had been pushing her for nearly two hours to walk slowly, painstakingly, along the path she had taken that fateful Saturday night before on her way home.

What they had seen gave them almost no hope at all—at best a distant chimney or the top of a neighbor's barn. Chilmark was not chock-a-block full of people. Fewer than five hundred souls, and spread out. Farms could be as small as forty acres, and as large as Nickerson's.

Merry stopped walking suddenly. She threw up her hands and collapsed on the wet ground, leaning back on her elbows.

" ~ Merry, you can't give up! ~ " Simon knelt beside his friend, his eyes darkening with concern. He took a swipe at his forehead and pushed back his damp brown hair. " ~ Try to think of something else that might help you, ~ " he urged.

" ~ Anything at all you remember. What happened when you left the store? What did you see? ~ "

Merry closed her eyes and tried to concentrate. When she opened them, they were blank. She looked at Simon and saw that he really quite resembled his cousin Spaulding. She smiled a little to herself, thinking of Eleanor and Spaulding in love.

" ~ What? ~ " Simon asked impatiently. " ~ Why are you smiling? ~ "

Merry shook her head. Then suddenly she sat up straight in the grass and grabbed Simon's arm. Simon did not move, waiting. ~ When I left, a man was coming in. ~

" ~ What man? Who? Mr. Fisher announced the names of all the men standing inside. Is this someone else? ~ "

Merry nodded eagerly.

" ~ Well, who? ~ "

~ I don't know. I'd never seen him before. ~

" ~ You mean he wasn't from around here? ~ "

Merry agreed.

" ~ How do you know? ~ "

~ Well, for one thing, his weskit. ~

" ~ What about it? ~ "

~ It was colored. Woven. Even in the dark I could see it had red and blue and bright green in it. It was fancy. ~

Simon scowled, puzzled.

~ Don't you understand, Simon? He couldn't have been from around here. He couldn't even have been from the island, unless it was Edgartown. *We* don't wear those colors! ~

" ~ Store-bought, probably. ~ "

~ Fancy clothes when you're all alone? ~ Merry wondered. ~ I bet even in Edgartown no one dresses like that. ~

" ~ I don't understand you, ~ " Simon said plainly, slumping onto the grass beside her now.

~ Simon, we—Up-islanders—the people who live *here*, we

wear browns and grays and maybe dark blue on special occasions. But this man was wearing a bright vest and white—well, no, not white—tan trousers. Now, stop and think, you work in the fields, you fish or farm, are you going to wear something that shows dirt? ~

" ~ No, ~ " Simon admitted, " ~ but I might wear something like that to church. ~ "

~ Maybe, but evensong was long over. No, this man didn't belong here. ~

Simon thought a moment before standing up and reaching back down to help Merry to stand, as well. " ~ Well, if he was a stranger, he wouldn't have any reason to kill Mr. Nickerson, would he? ~ "

Merry hugged herself a moment, twisting from side to side slightly in thought. ~ I bet Mr. Fisher doesn't know about this man, about how he was there that night. ~

" ~ If he was there, someone else would have seen him. ~ " Merry nodded her head eagerly.

" ~ But surely we would have heard something about this man, wouldn't we, if other people remembered him, too? ~ "

Merry shrugged. ~ Maybe people didn't think it was important. If you don't think the man had reason to kill Mr. Nickerson, why would anyone else think so? ~

Simon himself now shrugged, a little at sea. " ~ Everyone thinks the murderer must be someone who knew Mr. Nickerson. It just doesn't make sense otherwise. ~ "

~ But we don't know who knew Mr. Nickerson, or who did business with him. Maybe he cheated a provisioner from New Bedford or Plymouth who came to force him to pay what he owed. Maybe the man came to sell him something more. We *don't* know, don't you see? ~

Simon frowned. " ~ Does your father remember this man? He was at the store. Has he said anything? ~ "

~ No. But I bet that's only because he's thinking the same

way everyone else is, that the killer had to be someone from here who knew and hated Mr. Nickerson. ~

" ~ I don't know. . . . ~ "

~ Simon, answer me straight. Eleanor said she couldn't imagine Gerry Daggett sober and angry enough to do it. Henrietta Chapell is too dim. Mr. West is clearly too good a man. That left me. Is that what you think, too, down deep? ~

" ~ Never! ~ "

thirteen

~ Yes, that's true. ~

Simon beamed. Seated at the big table in the Skiffe kitchen along with the rest of Merry's family, her father had just confirmed what Merry had told him. " ~ Well then, sir, ~ " Simon sounded triumphant, " ~ all we have to do is tell Mr. Fisher! ~ "

" ~ That a visitor entered the store one night? ~ " asked Merry's mother, Molly. " ~ Simon, that's really not news, is it? ~ "

"Not to me, it isn't," Pickup announced.

"Shh," Bailey warned. "This is serious."

~ Nothing's going to happen to Merry, ~ Benjamin Skiffe declared.

" ~ The trouble is, Simon, ~ " Molly Skiffe added, " ~ if I were a constable, and the father of a suspect came to me with this kind of information—cloudy, is what I mean— I think I'd naturally regard it as . . . as self-serving. What father wants to see this happen to his child? ~ "

" ~ But there were other people inside, ~ " Simon argued.
" ~ Mr. Skiffe said so himself. ~ "

Ben Skiffe nodded.

" ~ Then all we need is for someone else to agree with you! ~ " Simon decided.

Molly smiled softly. She spoke as much to her husband and daughter as to Simon. " ~ The same thing holds true, dear, ~ " she said. " ~ People from Edgartown are likely to think all of us are protecting our own. Not only Merry, but Peter West and the others, as well. And in another case, that might be true. ~ "

~ Nothing bad will happen to Merry, ~ Ben Skiffe said again. ~ Trust me, Simon. We won't let it. ~

Merry sat silently between her sister and Simon, damp and chilled, feeling every moment less hope. If her mother could argue Simon away, what chance was there of persuading a grown-up? That her father had repeated his vow to protect her seemed natural and loving, but unless he had some sort of plan to help, what good was it?

Simon slumped in his chair. " ~ I don't understand, ma'am, ~ " he said. " ~ We know Merry had nothing to do with this. How can you argue that despite what we know, she might have? ~ "

" ~ That's not what I'm doing, Simon, ~ " Merry's mother replied. " ~ We know how serious this is. If we can imagine what others think, we can find some way to change their way of thinking. ~ "

"Devil's advocate," Bailey said softly to Simon.

"What does that mean?" he asked.

"That the best way to beat the devil is to play him, to pretend to be him, and to try to think as he would," Bailey explained.

Simon shook his head. He looked imploringly at Merry.

" ~ Do you think Mr. Fisher would think the way your mother says? ~ "

Sadly Merry nodded.

Without saying ~ Thank you ~ to Simon for everything he was trying to do, Merry stood at her place and then turned to leave the room. Her family could hear her slow tread on the stairs that encased the fireplace and chimney. They sat silently listening as her footsteps filtered down to them from the loft above.

As Molly offered Simon another cup of tea, Merry knelt upstairs and pulled out her suitcase.

She felt tired, so tired. And alone.

She knew her family would not abandon her, but in the face of their clear-thinking, she had realized that she would have to do what she most feared: run away. What mattered now was not bringing more sadness on the household. Sadness and shame.

She opened her suitcase and pulled out her notebook. Idly she looked at the pages on which she had drawn wildlife and flowers. She did not smile with recognition or regret. She leafed through until she came to her single diary entry. Then she pulled up her bottle of India ink and a sharp pen.

Tuesday, October 5, 1880

I am a good girl. I am and now I don't know what to do. Mr Fisher doesn't look like a mean man but I can't remember that he smiled at me this morning when he met me.

She sat back on her heels and looked at the words before her. She rested her head on her bed and closed her eyes again. She wished somehow she were more like her cousin. Eleanor was so brave and so determined. It didn't matter to her what people thought, about anything. To leave the island—which to Merry would be the greatest sadness of her life—with Spaulding Mayhew was madness, and yet Eleanor was ready to do so.

Merry's eyes opened wide. Suddenly she had two ideas, two wonderful thoughts that were so exciting she could hardly slow her mind enough to examine them.

It was true Eleanor was selfish. But down deep Merry still believed her cousin would come to her aid—as long as this did not mean upsetting her plans to take flight with Spaulding.

And there was no reason why Merry couldn't leave Chilmark with Eleanor and Spaulding!

The brightness that lit Merry's heart for a second dimmed almost as quickly. Eleanor and Spaulding were going to flee on Thursday night, when the fair ended, when the dancing ended and the displays were pulled down. Clearly they meant to stay the night in Vineyard Haven with one of Spaulding's friends before boarding the steamer that would carry them back across the Sound. That was two nights away, forty-eight hours off. What would she do in the meantime?

At a loss, Merry closed her notebook and rose up to her knees to lean over her bed. She closed her eyes again, the better to concentrate.

She would go to Eleanor in the morning to tell her what she planned. She was certain Eleanor would approve. After all, they had been best friends for so many years, how could she refuse?

And Merry had always liked Spaulding. Not as much as Eleanor, of course, but enough. At least she didn't dislike him, and she was willing to believe that in his heart he felt kindly towards her cousin.

Merry would present Eleanor with her plan. It was simple

and easy. Merry would run and hide; she would take food from the kitchen downstairs and find some place secure and hidden by bushes or trees or rocks. She would wait until dark on Thursday and then emerge to join Eleanor and Spaulding at whatever secret place *they* were meeting.

Merry would promise not to be any extra trouble to the pair, even promise that when they were quit of Martha's Vineyard, she, Merry, would say good-bye too to her cousin. Eleanor and Spaulding could go on their way freely and Merry would just do the best she could on her own.

She simply needed a little of Eleanor's courage to get started.

Merry's lips curled ever so slightly in the shadows of the loft. Good: she liked her plan, although she hated the thought of going to the mainland. But she had no choice.

She would get up in the middle of the night, steal downstairs and fill her suitcase with bread and cold meats. She would slip away into the dark before sunup and be at Eleanor's at dawn. She would hide somewhere nearby, careful to keep out of sight of all three Norton boys and Uncle Jeb when they began their day's chores.

It would take only a moment to speak with Eleanor and then she would steal away again to her hideout. And on Friday morning, when the early steamer pulled away from the dock, they would all run on board at the last minute and sail across the sound, there to part and start life anew.

And then what? Merry closed her eyes for a second and felt tears in them. Where would she go? Whom did she know?

With a great effort, Merry concentrated. Miraculously, a name floated into her mind. Miss Beach! In Hartford!

Almost as quickly as she opened her eyes in relief, Merry was downcast. She couldn't expect Miss Beach to hide her, not indefinitely. She couldn't work at the Asylum for too many people knew her and would report her presence back to her family. And if her family discovered where she was, so too would the Law.

Well, still . . . it was a goal, a safe haven for a few days or even hours. Miss Beach would help her, would think of something that she, Merry, could not. Merry could not imagine now what that something might be, but it was enough to kindle a taper to accompany her first independent steps.

Relieved, excited but also very, very tired, Merry crawled atop her bed, putting her suitcase and notebook down on the floor nearby.

Bailey found her breathing deeply and asleep an hour later. She covered Merry lightly and shushed Pickup. She pushed Merry's suitcase under the bed again and then saw the notebook.

Saying nothing to Pickup, Bailey put the journal between an elbow and her side and slipped out of the loft to tiptoe downstairs. Silently she went to the big table and lit just one candle so as not to startle her parents in their own small chamber.

She opened Merry's book and thumbed through its pages. She admired her sister's talent to draw and color, and wished she had the same ability. Then she came upon Merry's long entry dated the day before.

Bailey bent over the notebook, her blonde hair falling on either side of her face, to read.

At the end of the entry, Bailey looked up sorrowfully. How sweet and how alone poor Merry was, no matter how loved.

She shook her head. It was strange how well Merry spelled and wrote, but had no one in Hartford ever explained what punctuation was and how it worked?

Then, after a second's thought, she understood. As

Merry had written, as she had become more excited and determined to write what she imagined might prove her blameless, she had lost sight of what she had learned in Hartford. Short, direct sentences. No frills. No sentences with an endless stream of and's and so's and but's.

Bailey smiled sympathetically. She closed her sister's notebook. She felt just the tiniest bit guilty at having read what it contained, but also glad she had. She had never doubted her sister's innocence. Now she would be able to explain to the sheriff's deputy and anyone else who questioned exactly what Merry had done that fatal night.

Bailey would ask Merry the next morning to let her, Bailey, speak for her to the Law.

fourteen

Merry's eyes opened slowly. It was still so dark she could not make out the heavy beams that striped the ceiling above her. She held her breath as she leaned up on an elbow to peer at the beds of Bailey and Pickup. She squinted. There was no movement apart from slow breathing.

Knowing she would have to slip out of bed like a shadow herself, she sat up all the way and swung her feet beneath her covers towards the left. Her feet reached down and felt for her shoes.

Merry spent ten seconds blaming herself for not thinking further ahead. She should have put clothing aside the night before. She should have selected warm dark things, like a shawl or a skirt, the better to hide in the dark as long as she needed. The better to cross the landscape she imagined in her mind, from her hideout to wherever Eleanor and Spaulding were to meet. How awful to spend a whole night out-of-doors hiding and running only to be seen as she made a dash for her friends.

Ten seconds was all the time Merry had. She lifted her shoes, knotted their laces and slipped them over her head. She stood ever so slowly. She looked back. Neither Bailey nor Pickup had stirred. She ached to have a candle.

She reached out in the dark towards the bar from which hung her own and Bailey's clothes. Guessing and praying at the same time, she pulled down two garments and threw them over her arm.

In the kitchen below, after an inch-by-inch descent, Merry had to make choices the same way—blindly. She felt about in the larder and then wrapped part of a loaf of bread, some apples, and something that felt like cold meat in the dress she held. Knowing the island as she did, and being so familiar with what it grew natively, Merry decided she wouldn't need more than these few potables. She could survive on what she found in the woods.

She left no note. She hesitated, but finally decided there wasn't time. Who knew when another Skiffe might arise? How would she explain herself, caught in the middle of the kitchen, her cape on her shoulders, ready to bolt?

The air outside her door was gentle and damp. The cold of the season seemed to be holding off-island purposely. Merry was grateful. To the east, towards Edgartown, Merry thought the day was beginning to erase the stars above.

There was no time to think sad thoughts, or to grow tearful. On tiptoe at first, then running pell mell as she had after Simon had warned her two days before, she fled from the farmhouse.

fifteen

~ What are you doing here? ~

Merry pulled Eleanor around the corner of the Norton privy. She signalled urgency and secrecy. Eleanor's eyes, so recently scratchy with crumbles of heavy sleep, widened, but she allowed Merry to tug at her.

While she had been waiting for Eleanor to appear, hidden less than fifty feet from the Norton home in a stand of fog-shrouded black oak, Merry had made changes in her plan. She was desperate not to allow Eleanor the chance to deny her.

~ Where are you and Spaulding going to meet? On Thursday? ~

Eleanor's lips tipped upwards. ~ Behind the cattle shed, ~ she replied, excitement and romance returning to her face at the same time.

~ When? ~

~ Why? ~

~ I'll tell you in a minute. What time? ~

~ Well, ~ Eleanor began slowly, ~ first I'm to slip away from my father. Then, as soon as I can, I'm supposed to edge into the trees behind the cattle shed. I wait until I see Spaulding and then signal. He'll come to take my hand and then, I guess, together we'll rush off towards our new life. ~

~ But what time? ~ Merry asked insistently.

Eleanor shrugged. ~ Whenever the fair ends. ~

Merry nodded. ~ Fine. I'll meet you there, too. ~

~ What are you talking about? ~

~ Eleanor, I can't stay here! Mr. Fisher wants to put me to a test at noon today, what kind I don't know. But I cannot do it. I cannot shame my family. I have to escape. I have to leave. I'll go with you and Spaulding. ~

It was hard for Merry to ignore the fall of Eleanor's face. But rather than give her cousin the chance to argue, she rushed on. ~ I promise I won't hinder you. I promise that as soon as we're off the island, I'll go my own way. But, Eleanor, you must let me come with you! You must! You're my best friend. You're my only hope! ~

For the first time, Eleanor noticed the bundle under Merry's arm. ~ But what are you going to do between then and now? Hide? ~

Merry nodded quickly. ~ I'll find some little hillock or cave or somewhere I won't be seen and I'll wait until tomorrow when we meet. ~

~ But your family— ~

~ I know, I know. They'll be frantic searching. Better that though than living with the shame of a murderer. ~

Eleanor took a quick pace backwards. ~ Are you that? ~

~ Of course I'm not! That you could even think that way, even ask that question, just proves how little hope I would have if I stayed here. Eleanor, don't be angry with me. Don't forbid me. For all the years of our lives together, let me escape with you and Spaulding. I'll never after trouble you. ~

Eleanor looked down, a frown forming, as she wrapped her mother's angora shawl more tightly about her body. When she looked up, prepared to tell Merry what she thought of the plan, Merry had disappeared.

sixteen

Merry felt very pleased with herself. Rather than running farther from home and Eleanor's farm, she turned southeast, skirting the boundaries of stone walls that kept the Norton stock from ranging down to the salt marshes near the sea. Then she cut north, slipping between clumps of helpful scrub oak and white pine, to creep around her very own homestead.

Once past view of her own house, Merry changed directions again and ran east, towards Edgartown. But this direction held her interest only for a short while. Once more, she dodged towards the south and came, sooner than she had imagined, to the head of Tisbury Great Pond where two fingerlike inlets of brackish water crept northwards towards the island's center.

She ran right down the vee formed by the watery branches. As the sun rose more fully above her, breathlessly she pressed through and past highbush blueberrys and swamp azaleas, past pepperbushes and wild grapes. Knowing the water in the pond to be salty, a result of the ocean's breech of South Beach last winter, Merry tried to remember where each wild grapevine grew so she could return to strip stems of any fruit that remained so late in the season. She hadn't, after all, brought water with her and October could sometimes hold the exhausting heat of the summer.

As she pushed through the bracken and cinnamon ferns that told her she was nearing the water itself, she smiled to recall that in the dark, just a few hours ago, she had accidentally grabbed one of Bailey's very best Sunday dresses to take with her. She doubted Bailey would be angry, since her sister had always been generous with anything she owned. Still and all, it was going to be a shock for her.

Feeling the first strong rays of the sun and happy to sense her dew-dampened clothes begin to dry, Merry estimated the time to be about eight, maybe eight-thirty. By this time, the alarm would have been sounded. Her family would be up and confused, looking everywhere for her. She imagined her father asking neighbors to help in the search. And she felt unaccountably proud at the cleverness of her flight.

True, there was not a lot of natural outcrop or cover behind which to hide, let alone here on the edge of the marsh a dry cave or hummock in which to sleep later, but what there was—fledgling juneberry trees, red maple and tupelo—gave cover enough.

She was startled then and almost immediately pleased by the sudden arrival of half a dozen redwing blackbirds near her. If only she could hear their song, she thought, they could have acted as alarms. Well, their flight and dives and sudden risings from the marsh grasses would do the very same thing.

The sun rose higher in the sky and Merry realized she was hungry, hot, and beginning to be sleepy. She collapsed in a bed of ferns, those her neighbors called "sensitive" ferns because they couldn't stand the harsh winters on the island. In high summer, they were lush and rather soft on which to sit, easily crushed, giving off a pleasant scent.

She shrugged off her cape and opened the small satchel of food she had carried since dawn. She reached down to check her stores and was surprised to find that what had felt like cold meat in the darkness at home turned out now to be a slab of homemade goat cheese.

She selected an apple and painstakingly, as she had often watched Ezra do, put her fingers on either side of its top, near the stem. She pulled quickly and the apple opened easily, as though it were a flower unfolding for her inspection. With a finger, she took some of the goat cheese and spread it on one-half of the apple and ate it. The blend of tastes was new to her but she liked it.

She looked around where she had chosen to rest. She doubted any of the search party, no matter how large, would look for her in the marshes near Tisbury Pond, but it paid to take precautions. She reached out to pull by the roots some of the ferns around her, piling the fronds up one by one in a cross-hatch pattern to make a wall through which it might be difficult to see. She squinched on her bottom across a few feet, taking her fern-screen with her, so that her back rested against the frailish trunk of baby tupelo. Not much shade was provided by its young branches, but she could hang Bailey's dress in such a way that shade covered her head and face.

Satisfied that she was as protected from prying eyes as possible, Merry stretched out on her cape and beneath Bailey's skirt. She could look past its edge into the blue sky above. Occasionally a blackbird darted across her vision. Once an egret, white and thin as a beam of sunlight in a forest, flashed by overhead.

She put her hands behind her head and sighed. She prayed Eleanor, if questioned, would say nothing. For her to do so would mean that Eleanor's elopement might be discovered and stopped. Besides, no one had seen them talking that morning. Eleanor, unlike her cousin, was good at "social fibbing."

Merry closed her eyes against the sunlight that filtered through Bailey's cotton. She was proud of herself. She had made a plan and carried it out.

Idly, Merry waved away a fly that hovered near her mouth. Then again she put her hand behind her head and settled into the comfortable bed of ferns she had fashioned, closing her eyes once more. I can do this. I can do this. I *can* do this.

And, hearing, she might have.

seventeen

Lucy and Bedford Vincent, whose family owned the land at the top of Tisbury Pond all the way to up to the Takemmy Trail, weren't really serious about collecting chicory root for their mother. At nine years and seven, neither drank the coffee that was sometimes distilled after roasting the chicory root.

They idled almost aimlessly down towards the eastern fork of the pond that snaked up into their property. They had been sent on this errand more as a means of keeping them out of the way of their mother's busy nursing than because of anything anyone back home wanted to drink. The Vincent children were having a bout of measles. Lucy and Bedford had recovered, but were not yet allowed to return to their studies at their tiny one-room school.

They knew why they had been sent out-of-doors. Even their black-and-white setter, Fletcher, seemed to know that his airing was more to please his masters than for real exercise. He didn't bother to run ahead and then dash back to see what he had missed. He ambled ahead of the children by only a few feet and, when they stopped, he did, sinking gratefully onto the ground in whatever shade he could find.

Together the Vincents swiped at the sailor-blue flowers on the tall chicory plants, and smiled to see the square-tip blossoms float off as though they were aging dandelions. Bedford, the more serious of the pair, occasionally would pull up a plant and trail it along after him just so that when he returned home he wouldn't be scolded. Lucy didn't care at all.

The sun was well up, and the day was going to be still and warm after yesterday's storm. Redwing blackbirds rose and fell lazily from their perches on tall grasses as the two Vincents progressed. Fletcher ignored their flights. Had they been pheasant or bobwhite, he would have gone berserk.

The faint rose color of Bailey's cotton dress would not, by itself, have aroused much interest in Fletcher. But it moved. Not a lot, just a little, as though a tiny breeze were a gentle wave eddying around the last rock on a beach at low tide.

Fletcher stirred slowly, pushing his strong shoulders through the underbrush. He stopped about five feet from the dress itself and stared a moment. He looked back once at the Vincents before giving an almost disinterested bark. Then he sank again onto the ground, put his head on his forepaws, and kept the pink cotton under watch.

Lucy and Bedford walked unhurriedly towards their dog and stopped inches behind his tail. After a moment, Bedford took a few silent steps and peered under the rose-colored tent that shaded Merry.

The run back up to their farmhouse took less than fifteen minutes.

eighteen

Bailey lifted her dress from the grass and began carefully to fold it as her father carried the still-sleeping Merry to place her gently in the back of his trap. The healthy portion of the Vincent family stood silently watching, not more than twenty feet away.

Bailey climbed up to sit beside her father who, as he turned Back-'n'-Fill carefully around through the underbrush, nodded to the Vincents. ~ Thank you. ~

~ You let us know how things go, Ben, ~ Hiram Vincent counselled. ~ We know the poor thing had nothing to do with any of this business. ~

Benjamin Skiffe nodded again and bounced his reins atop Back-'n'-Fill's backside. The horse began slowly to pull away on a path that ran towards the road.

It was the motion rather than the hardness of the wood beneath her that woke Merry.

At first she was confused, still dazed from her nap. Then she sat straight up and looked around. She couldn't see the

Vincents for the trees that now separated the trap from the bottom of the farm property. How could this have happened?

On the front seat ahead of her, Bailey turned around. ~ How did you find me? ~ Merry asked, now sad and disappointed in herself. There was something she had not done, something she had not thought of.

" ~ The Vincents came and told us, ~ " Bailey explained.

~ But how did they know? ~

" ~ Little Bedford and his sister found you. ~ "

Merry dropped her eyes. What shame.

Bailey reached out to touch Merry's hair. " ~ It'll be fine, Merry. We're glad they found you. ~ "

Merry stared silently at her sister.

" ~ After all, you gave us a fright, ~ " Bailey continued. " ~ We alerted everyone we knew. Mr. Vincent heard about you. ~ "

~ Are we going home? ~

Bailey shook her head and tried hard to look encouraging even as she told Merry the bad news. " ~ It's not far from noon, dear. We must go to the store. You remember. Mr. Fisher wants to see you. ~ "

Merry jumped to her knees and reached out for her father's shoulder. He turned quickly to look over his shoulder. ~ Stop! ~ Merry commanded. ~ Stop! We can't go any further! I can't go to the store! ~

Wrapping Back-'n'-Fill's reins loosely around one of the wooden armrests on the trap, her father tried to comfort Merry. ~ We must, my dear. I promised that we would. You have nothing to fear. ~

Back-'n'-Fill slowed his pace but did not stop.

~ But I don't know that! ~ Merry argued. ~ We don't know what trick he has in mind! ~

~ Mr. Fisher seems like a fair man to me, and a good one, ~ Ben Skiffe offered.

" ~ Besides, Merry, we have to go see him, ~ " Bailey said. " ~ We have to tell him about the stranger who came to the post office that night. ~ "

~ But Mama said he wouldn't believe us! ~

Bailey remembered. " ~ I think she's wrong. Especially if other people who were there that night agree with us, if they too recall seeing the man. ~ "

Merry knew she could argue no further. She turned quickly, preparing to jump to the ground. Bailey reached out more quickly and grabbed Merry's arm. She held it tightly.

If Merry jumped, her arm would be broken. Bailey's grip was firm. Merry looked up at her sister and saw determination on her face.

Merry sank back, resigned. Bailey did not release her.

Suddenly Merry remembered a picture she had seen in a book of French men and women being carted to their deaths at the guillotine.

nineteen

This terrifying image stayed in her mind as her father steered the trap past the general store/post office and made a left turn, to tie up at the side of the clapboarded building.

Bailey still held Merry's arm firmly, but she had also slipped off the bench in front to kneel beside her. Both stared back at their neighbors and friends who examined them as they passed.

Merry was stunned by the size of the crowd. Rather than hold whatever sort of meeting this was to be within the walls of Mr. Mayhew's store, Mr. Fisher stood tall and dark, and serious, on the front steps of the building. Merry dropped her eyes and closed them. He looked so forbidding, almost as she would have imagined God standing sternly at the gates of heaven.

The carriage halted and Benjamin Skiffe jumped down to tie up Back-'n'-Fill. No one in the crowd came forward or tried to embrace Merry. Instead, the men and women and older children stood silently, waiting, watching. A few people began to edge slyly towards the front steps of the store, to stand in a clump at the feet of Mr. Fisher who did not greet the Skiffes in any way other than a curt nod.

Bailey helped Merry off the back of the cart and held her hand tightly as they began to walk towards Mr. Fisher. Merry was fighting inwardly. She wanted no one to see her. She felt as though she were in one of her own nightmares. But she also knew exactly where she was and while she couldn't have known what to expect, she did know she had to give a good account of herself.

She tried to keep her eyes demurely on the ground in front of her as she walked, but she was too curious. She looked up twice, once relieved in an odd way to see Gerry Daggett at one side and just below Mr. Fisher, looking as though at any moment he might collapse from nerves and fright. Strangely, this gave her confidence.

So she looked up the second time, now rather boldly, to see Peter West and his wife, Marjorie, standing at the other side of Mr. Fisher.

Peter West's face was serene, his eyes untroubled. His hair had been neatly watered and parted on the left, and he had freshly shaved. Marjorie clutched her husband's arm in alarm. Merry could almost feel her fingernails slicing through her husband's jacket.

There was a long, terribly silent moment then—as Bailey and Merry, with their father behind them, stopped walking and stood at the bottom of the stairs just below Mr. Fisher. No one knew what might happen next and almost every breath was being held until, finally, Mr. Fisher nodded his acknowledgment, and the crowd sighed gratefully, relieved.

Sixty people moved closer to the center of the scene, still keeping a good distance away from its principal players. Merry looked around, panicked, and short of breath. She leaned weakly back into Bailey's arms.

A hand from somewhere reached out and touched Merry's.

She nearly leapt from her skin. It was Simon, looking cock-sure and very important, truant. " ~ I already told him, ~ " he said.

Merry couldn't imagine what Simon meant.

" ~ About the stranger, ~ " Simon explained insistently. " ~ The man you saw as you left. ~ "

"Did he believe you?" asked Bailey in a whisper.

" ~ He had to, for old Jedediah Pease said that he, too, remembered the man. And then a couple of others thought about it, and they, too, remembered. ~ "

~ What did they remember? ~ Merry asked but weakly, not daring to hope.

Simon suddenly grinned. Merry couldn't think why. " ~ He was toyed with. ~ "

" ~ What do you mean? ~ " Bailey demanded.

" ~ Well, the stranger came in and everyone there, in the post office, knew he wasn't from around here. Sometimes, you know, people like to tease. I guess the man was lost and needed directions. But since he wasn't an Islander, people decided to play a joke. No one answered his questions at all. ~ "

" ~ That's very rude, ~ " Bailey decided.

" ~ Come on, Bailey, you've done it yourself. ~ "

" ~ Never, ~ " Bailey said, but she blushed.

~ What happened? ~ Merry demanded.

Simon giggled. " ~ Everyone drew himself up. It was dark but for one lamp, you see, and there were a lot of shadows. Everyone tried to look dour and threatening. And then they all began to speak, in sign. Whether or not they could hear didn't make any difference. They teased this poor man by making him think they had a secret language. Every time he asked a question, people answered him in sign. The fellow was so confused that after a while he just turned and ran away. ~ "

Mr. Fisher cleared his throat. He needn't have bothered, for simply by opening his mouth he had the attention of the entire crowd. "May we begin, ladies and gentlemen?"

As he spoke, he did not ask for anyone to help his neighbor understand. Perhaps in his few days in Chilmark he had come to understand that those who could hear would automatically assist those who couldn't.

Bailey translated for Merry and her father.

"'Tis after noon, and time to begin," Mr. Fisher announced. "We have before us those citizens of Chilmark who—either by their own admission or the report of their families or neighbors—do not have alibis or witnesses as to their whereabouts on Saturday last, the night of the murder of Mr. Edward Nickerson."

No one needed to have the citizens cited named.

"What I have in mind," Mr. Fisher continued, coming down the steps to stand on the flat ground before the store, "is a physical test. We believe Mr. Nickerson met his untimely death at the hands of another, and we believe that this was the murder weapon."

He pointed at his feet and there, until that very moment ignored by everyone, was a large piece of field granite, jagged and edged, weighing what looked to be nearly thirty pounds. The blood of Ned Nickerson still stained its sharpest point.

Merry looked down.

And then she fainted.

twenty

Bailey reached out as quickly as she could, and Ben Skiffe took a step forward instantly. Merry was not allowed to sink onto the ground in a swoon.

The flock that surrounded them "ooo-ed" and gasped, and itself took half a step forward.

Mr. Fisher walked forward to join the Skiffe family. "Is she all right?" he asked.

Bailey nodded, although uncertain. Merry's eyes were still closed and her body limp.

"Put her on the ground," suggested the deputy.

Benjamin Skiffe was doing that on his own, ever so gently taking Merry from Bailey's arms and delicately allowing his daughter a moment of peace stretched out atop the thin grass in front of the general store.

After a moment more, Merry opened her eyes. She looked puzzled, partly because she was looking straight up into the noon sun. She shielded her eyes as she leaned up unsteadily on one elbow to look around. Then she remembered everything.

She wanted so badly to sink again into forgetfulness. She had felt, for just a fraction of a second, as though she had had the most delightful dreamless sleep. To be awakened back into this nightmare should have been someone else's wretched fate.

Bailey had out her handkerchief and fanned Merry's feverish face, into which her natural color was returning. As though every limb ached with flu, Merry slowly brought her legs under her and, using Benjamin as a crutch, stood shakily once again before Mr. Fisher.

Mr. Fisher looked somberly down at Merry and then, to everyone's surprise, he smiled encouragingly. "Are you feeling stronger?" he asked almost in a whisper.

Bailey had barely started to relay his question before Merry nodded. In a way she felt she had disappointed Mr. Fisher. She gave him a weak smile.

Mr. Fisher nodded then and took half a dozen paces back. Once more he cleared his throat.

As he spoke, Merry stared at the stone lying in front of her. The noon sun made Mr. Nickerson's blood seem almost black. How could it, his blood, the stone, still seem shiny after all this time? She shivered. It was as though the stone had a life of its own, an evil one.

"Ladies and gentlemen," Mr. Fisher repeated, "I have asked you here to witness a test."

The crowd moved slightly closer. Simon Mayhew now stood directly beside Merry. He wanted to reach out to hold her hand, but in full view he dared not.

"This is the stone that was used in the terrible murder of Mr. Edward Nickerson, Saturday last. What we will see this afternoon is whether each or any of these people before us could have lifted the stone and hurled it at the victim."

The intrigued crowd murmured softly, seeming to think this was a good idea.

"In order to seem fair in this ordeal, I propose that each man or woman lift the stone and throw it, however they will or can. We shall ask that this be done in alphabetical order, beginning with Miss Chapell."

Merry had never before seen Henrietta Chapell and, but for the weight of the present moment, would hardly have noticed her if she had.

Henny Chapell was barely more than a girl, older than Bailey but not by much. Her chestnut hair fell only to her shoulders, and the darkness of her skirt and cap seemed to draw every bit of natural color from her face. She looked neither lively nor fetching, despite her youth. She stood very straight, although she was not tall; her features were composed and serious. She was a plain young woman, perhaps pleasant but plain.

She took a step from the edges of the circle that surrounded Mr. Fisher and then stopped abruptly, her posture indicating that that was as far as she was prepared to go.

Mr. Fisher nodded a greeting, but Henny Chapell did not return it. Rather than accept courtesy from the man from Edgartown, Henny averted her eyes from him to scan those of her neighbors. When she spoke, her voice rang with surprising clarity and firmness.

"If you wish to charge me," she said, "I shall go with you."

"I cannot force you, Miss Chapell," said Mr. Fisher seriously. "I can only advise you that to be cooperative at this time might well stand you in eventual good stead."

Henrietta Chapell nodded in agreement. "Well it might were I accused of anything." She turned away from Mr. Fisher and spoke directly to the crowd. "Where I was last Saturday night is no one's business but my own. Where I worked until a few months ago is already known. Why I no longer work in that house is a reason I refuse to divulge."

Most people in the circle around Mr. Fisher stared at Henny Chapell blankly. A few nodded somberly. She might not have been the prettiest girl up-island, but as far as anyone knew she was honest. Some secretly had wondered, when her departure from her last post had become known, whether she was also brave.

Mr. Fisher coughed, and then he purposely turned his cough into a lighter sound, quite resembling that of pleasant laughter. "None of us doubts," he said next, smiling at Henny Chapell, "that you have led a godly life, Miss Chapell. And you are, presently, accused of nothing more than doing whatever it was you did Saturday last privately, as is your right. I do hope, however, that you will hold yourself available to be questioned at a later date, should any member of a court find this to be a salutary thing."

Henny Chapell nodded severely. "Salutary for whom?" she asked.

A woman in the crowd behind her laughed appreciatively, but then fell silent as Henrietta Chapell broke through the ranks of onlookers to leave the site altogether, her stiff figure receding quickly as she stomped her way across a field towards her own lodging nearby.

Simon Mayhew took heart from Henrietta Chapell's stand. " ~ You can't expect Merry to lift that, either! ~ " he sputtered angrily.

"Why may I not?" asked Mr. Fisher patiently.

" ~ Well, look at her, for heaven's sakes! ~ " Simon directed. " ~ She's weak and thin and unwell. ~ "

Mr. Fisher nodded. He turned to look directly into Merry's eyes. Merry held his look. She wouldn't beg.

Without another word to Simon, Mr. Fisher looked next at Gerry Daggett. "Mr. Daggett, then, if you please," he said.

Gerry Daggett, trembling either with fear or in the grip of a horrendous hangover, took a step into the circle, closer to

82

the stone. He was dressed, days after his master's death, still in the Nickerson livery. Even at noon he wore his shining boots and driver's long-coat. He took off his top hat and laid it carefully at his feet. Then he looked up at Mr. Fisher, a question on his face.

"However you may," Mr. Fisher directed. "Whenever you are ready, simply lift the stone and throw it."

Gerry Daggett nodded that he understood. His bloodshot eyes focused on the stone, on the jagged edge so dark with blood. He bent to reach out with both hands. He lifted it without touching the natural fatal blade.

He stood a moment, unmoving. Then, with an effort that nearly pushed him back against the crowd, he heaved the stone outwards, away from his body.

The crowd gasped, and those in the circle nearest where the stone landed flinched quickly and moved back.

Gerry Daggett was sweating.

So was Merry. After "Daggett" came "Skiffe."

Without warning, Gerry Daggett's legs shook with both effort and relief and could no longer hold him upright. He fell hard onto his behind, his cream-colored britches absorbing the Chilmark dust. After a second, his body continued its downward pitch and he lay sprawled on his back, his eyes closed, his chin pointed into the sun.

Bernard Cleland emerged from the crowd and knelt beside his friend, taking off his wide-brimmed hat to fan Gerry's flushed face.

After a few moments, the attention of the crowd surrounding them shifted towards Mr. Fisher once more.

Mr. Fisher stood sternly watching and, assured that Gerry Daggett was not in peril of immediate demise, turned towards Benjamin Skiffe.

Merry's father understood the glance and put his hand on Merry's shoulder. He did not add pressure or push her forward. He didn't have to. On her own, Merry took the five steps across the circle and stood above the stone.

Despite her terror, she looked from the stone towards her father. Bailey and Simon stood on either side of Benjamin.

Merry felt torn. The stone looked impossibly heavy. It still looked murderous. If she lifted it, in a way it would be killing her, too.

Yet if she didn't, if she could not, might not her father be shamed?

" ~ Wait! Stop! ~ "

It was Simon again.

"Master Mayhew?" Mr. Fisher's tone was still patient.

" ~ This is unfair! ~ " Simon argued hotly. " ~ Gerry Daggett is nearly three score and a man. How dare you ask the same of a girl? There is not a way in the world Merry could lift that stone now or Saturday last. She's frail! ~ "

While a murmur of agreement began to rise from some of the onlookers, Merry reddened and without looking again at Simon, she bent from the waist, put her hands on the stone, and lifted it.

She held it before her for a second, as though the stone itself were nothing more than a serving tray. Then in one long movement that looked easy but which took every ounce of her strength, she hoisted the stone to arm's length above her head.

As though she were an avenging angel, angry and judging, she hurled the weight straight into the ground at her feet.

twenty-one

As though a shell from the War Between the States had long lain dormant and, without warning, exploded in the middle of an unsuspecting crowd, the Chilmark citizens who stood in a circle around Mr. Fisher and Merry Skiffe jumped back and cried out.

Merry was standing absolutely rigid, her eyes tightly clenched, her chin held up towards the sun in defiance.

A low buzz grew as people nearby turned to their neighbors. Suddenly there was no doubt: little Merry Skiffe could have killed Ned Nickerson. Whether or not she had actually done so was now less important than what the people had seen for themselves.

Merry took a big breath and opened her eyes. She stared straight up into the face of Mr. Fisher, who stood as though rooted in the island's sandy soil, stunned and a little uncertain about what he should do next.

Simon Mayhew had no such doubt. He reached out quickly for Merry's hand and squeezed it hard as he took a step back, drawing Merry in the same direction.

Benjamin Skiffe took a step forward, from the inner edge of the circle that had witnessed his daughter's deed. Glancing quickly and angrily at Mr. Fisher, he took two more steps and bent down quickly to lift the heavy stone himself. The crowd surrounding him jumped back quickly, unclear what to expect.

And as the citizens recoiled in expectation of they knew not what, Simon pulled Merry another few feet backwards. For a second the two were still in the circle of spectators. Then as people gaped silently to see Ben Skiffe bring the weight over his head, Simon gave one gigantic tug and pulled Merry through their neighbors and into open space.

Without explaining to her what he wanted, Simon turned and began to run, forcing Merry to follow. Before Ben Skiffe threw the stone to the ground in front of him, Simon and Merry were rounding the corner of the post office and heading for a line of oaks that cupped the old wooden building.

Fleeing into trees, Simon and Merry did not see Bailey Skiffe bend down to retrieve the stone, stand and bring it up over her head, and smash it into the dirt before her.

Peter West never had to prove he, too, might have been a murderer.

twenty-two

Simon would not let go of Merry's hand.

Surprised at first by his strength and determination, Merry allowed herself to be pulled along. But even as she ran, she was thinking: this is what I have to do but I cannot.

In the one great moment of decision so far in her life, Merry had faced fear and beaten it. What she felt now was simple exhaustion. Every resource she might have drawn upon had already been spent.

Simon yanked and pulled. As they reached the trees that formed a neat semicircle around the back of the store, he dropped into a crouch. He still had Merry's hand. She, too, was forced to bend down, below the sightline of the stone wall that separated the store property from the Poole farm.

There was only one way Merry could think to stop Simon. She fell.

Simon let go of Merry's hand and whirled around, kneeling to face her, his hands wild. " ~ Are you crazy? ~ " he demanded. " ~ We have to get out of here! ~ "

Merry shook her head simply.

" ~ You're wrong! After what you did—how could you do that? It was suicide! ~ "

Merry gave Simon a little crinkly smile. ~ It was your own fault. ~

" ~ Mine?! ~ "

Merry nodded. ~ You forced me. I am not, and never have been, a weak, fragile little girl. You finally saw that. ~

Simon stared at Merry for a moment. Then, apparently having made a decision of his own, he grabbed her hand and pulled her to her feet. With not another word, he set off again at a run, bent double, staying below the top of the stone walls to his right.

Merry hadn't the strength to fight Simon. She wanted desperately to stop running, to sit down and rest, to catch her breath, to lean against a wall and close her eyes and just have a few moments' peace.

Simon's grip hardened as he stopped suddenly, peeked around a gateway, and then spurted ahead, Merry in his wake, heading for an honest stand of pitch pine and white oak that stood darkly and safely nearly half a mile ahead.

Merry felt like a rag doll at the end of a string.

twenty-three

Simon was red-faced and breathless, but determined. He knew he was pulling an unwilling hostage, but it was for her own good. He cared for Merry, a lot. She was his friend. A young man should always be protective of the weaker sex.

At the end of his arm, Merry trailed. They had been dodging below walls, crashing through pines and white oak, never stopping for a moment to rest. The sun was still high above them and around them were no sounds but those of birds and a distant bleating of sheep.

Merry's feet seemed to her lighter than before. She followed her friend with an increasing sense of adventure rather than fear. She had done what she must and now it was up to God to make certain that her innocence was recognized despite the fact that she did have the strength to kill another human being. But who, she wondered, did not? In one way or another, with a tool or a stone, even a tiny child could extinguish the life of a tormentor.

Simon dropped suddenly to the ground, yanking Merry down nearly on top of him. Merry sat up and pulled slightly apart from her rescuer, looking puzzled.

" ~ We have to cross here, ~ " Simon announced, panting.

~ Where are we going? ~

" ~ Below Middle Road, towards the sea but not to it, if you know what I mean. ~ "

Merry shook her head. ~ I have no idea. I no longer even know why we're running away. ~

" ~ Trust me, ~ " Simon urged. " ~ After we get across the road, when we can hide somewhere, I'll tell you. ~ "

~ Tell me now. Then maybe we can stop. ~

But rather than speak, Simon stood up and peered through the thin scrubby trees that lined Middle Road. From his hiding place, he could see the dirt lane that ran down the island from Chilmark to West Tisbury. He looked one way and then another and saw no traffic, neither carriage nor cart, no peddler or citizen. But he knew that sooner rather than later they would be pursued.

He bent down and grabbed Merry's hand, forcing her to her feet. He had spotted a gap in the stone walls on the other side of the road, on property that belonged to his uncle. He hadn't decided whether or not to ask for safe haven from his own family but he felt relieved to see familiar territory.

Once more looking up and down the road, Simon nodded to himself, convinced that this was the moment. He stepped from the side of the road and began to hurtle across. Merry was forced to follow.

But Simon didn't stop when he had dashed through the stone gate. Instead he picked up his pace and together he and Merry ran across Frederick Mayhew's north field towards a cairn, a pile of fieldstone that acted as a landmark for the Mayhew flocks. On one side of it was a large salt box, placed at the edge of a pond for watering. Just below this, on the pool's far rim, lay a circular, untouched stand of heavy trees.

Simon did not stop running until he and Merry were deep within the shelter of nature. Finally he sank upon the ground, letting go of Merry's hand, stretching out on his stomach, trying to get a lungful of crisp, cleansing air.

Merry sat beside her friend, happy rather than not. She loved being surrounded by the shade. She imagined how the crows and blackbirds above them would call to one another in warning or greeting. She wished now that she had thought to bring her notebook and her pens with her.

She smiled to herself. But of course. She hadn't known . . . anything. She hadn't imagined throwing the stone; she hadn't thought about running from the store yard.

And everything she had thought of before—Bailey's dress, the food, her cape—lay where it had been put before going to meet Mr. Fisher: in the back of her father's trap.

Merry leaned back on her hands and stared up through the thinning leaves of the trees above her. Even though the day was warm, the trees hadn't been fooled. Winter was not so very far away. Leaves had begun to fall and settle. Some tree limbs were bare enough already to seem like dark lace against the bright heavens.

She would try to draw them thus . . . if . . . when she got . . .

twenty-four

" ~ You can't go home! ~ "

~ Whyever not? ~

" ~ Because now everyone in Chilmark knows how strong you are, how possible it is for you to have killed Ned Nickerson. ~ "

Merry shook her head, smiling a little. ~ All those people also saw Gerry Daggett throw the stone. Who knows, after we fled, maybe Peter West was able to do the same thing I did. ~

" ~ That won't matter, ~ " Simon scowled.

~ Of course it will. ~

Simon shook his head.

~ What about the man I saw that night, the man others remember now, too? ~

Simon closed his eyes in frustration. After a moment, he opened them again and began explaining, in the way that drove Merry to distraction, how he saw her situation.

" ~ They won't find him. And I'll tell you why. Suppose that man exists and that he really did kill Ned Nickerson. Suppose, as you imagine, he is from off-island. Do you think that man is still hanging about, waiting to be apprehended? He's had almost four whole days to get off the Vineyard. What on earth makes you think such a fellow would come forward, even to save you? ~ "

Merry stared at her friend. ~ I didn't think he would come forward to save me, ~ Merry countered. She thought a moment. ~ But this is a big island. Why wouldn't he be doing what we are—hiding until it's safe to leave? ~

" ~ I'll tell you why. Because he doesn't know his way around. He's a stranger. Someone would see him, someone who's heard about Nickerson's death. Now that people know an outsider was seen that night, any unfamiliar man will be suspect. Merry, that man has disappeared, I promise you. ~ "

~ Gerry Daggett hasn't disappeared. Nor Peter West. ~

Simon was growing impatient. " ~ Nor Henny Chapell. Nor must they. Gerry Daggett was kept alive by the wages Ned Nickerson paid him, and that probably accounts for Henny Chapell, as well. Peter West is a man of honor and property. ~ "

~ Am I not equally honorable? ~ Despite her conviction, Merry felt herself growing chill with renewed anxiety.

Simon sat silently a moment. He knew what he had to say, and he hated the words even before he uttered them. To speak of all this would make *him* seem less than honorable. They would make him seem like a spy.

He sighed.

" ~ You are, that I know. Because I saw it. ~ "

~ Saw what? ~ Now Merry was really alarmed.

" ~ I saw you and Ned Nickerson on the south shore. ~ "

Merry's eyes grew wide.

" ~ I know what I saw, Merry. You and Ned Nickerson, he reaching for your hand, you pulling away. ~ "

~ You were following me? Spying on me? ~

Simon shook his head vigorously. " ~ Never. All I was doing was coming down to the beach to look for you. ~ " Simon paused. " ~ What was Ned Nickerson saying to you, Merry? What made you pull and run from him? Why didn't he mount his horse to chase after you? ~ "

Merry dropped her eyes. She looked at her hands. She shrugged.

" ~ I think I know why, ~ " Simon admitted.

Merry looked up again, directly into Simon's blue eyes.

" ~ Because it didn't really matter to him that you denied him, ~ " Simon guessed. " ~ He had young girls enough already at Indian Hill. ~ "

Merry flushed and felt hot. She couldn't hold her look steady. She closed her eyes and hot tears seeped from her lids.

Simon reached over to put his hand on Merry's shoulder. He shook her gently until she opened her eyes again. " ~ No one else knows, Merry. I would never tell anyone, never. Believe me. ~ "

Merry wanted to believe him.

" ~ But, Merry, suppose *he* did. Suppose Ned Nickerson himself talked about what he'd wanted from you. Suppose he told someone else how you had denied him. Suppose he had decided to bide his time and try again. Suppose someone else knew that. ~ "

Merry went from hot to cold. She grew pale. Was Simon suggesting that Henny Chapell, a woman she did not even know, would do something so desperate to preserve Merry's name?

" ~ You can't go home, Merry. ~ "

~ What am I to do? ~ She remembered then her original plan, of meeting Eleanor and Spaulding at the fair and fleeing with them the next night. She ached to tell Simon about this but she couldn't. For Eleanor's sake. ~ What am I to do? ~

twenty-five

For a moment Simon said nothing. He couldn't think of what step to take next. He half-wanted to blame himself for this quandary, but he couldn't. He had acted to save his friend. No one, not even himself, would have expected him to look into the future to plan such a deed.

Simon shrugged, but he smiled. " ~ We'll think of something, ~ " he said reassuringly.

Merry, fearful but knowing that what Simon had forced her to do had come from his heart, nodded, trying to calm herself. She, too, tried a weak smile. ~ It's nice here. Whose place is this? ~

" ~ One of my uncles. I can go down to the house there, just beyond the garden wall, and get us food. ~ "

Merry wasn't hungry, but she remembered that she had left her supplies in the back of her father's trap. She would need food later, wherever she was. Then she had a sudden thought. ~ Simon, you can't stay here with me. ~

" ~ But why not? ~ "

~ Because your family will be looking for you. They'll be very concerned, you know. And you must go to school tomorrow. If you stay with me, people will understand we're both on the run. They'll know to look for two of us, rather than only one. ~

" ~ Let them, ~ " Simon said fiercely. He was very confident. " ~ They'll never catch us. Not if we're smart. ~ "

~ Simon, how smart can we be on an island? ~

Simon's eyes, full of pride and fire a second before, went blank.

~ After all, there are only so many places we could be, ~ Merry continued. She smiled at her own thought. ~ Even if we are sort of smallish people, easy to hide, people know us. You yourself told me that. ~

Merry felt strange. She was comforting Simon, explaining the way of the world to *him*. What she was doing to herself, deep inside, was confirming her own fear. Where could she hide, she alone?

Simon suddenly put his finger to his mouth. He reached out for Merry's shoulder and pushed her to the ground. Merry looked at him, puzzled.

" ~ A carriage, ~ " Simon whispered.

The two froze in place. While they were hidden by the stand of trees, they still weren't far from Middle Road that led towards West Tisbury. Although she couldn't hear the approaching wheels on the road behind her, Merry imagined that whoever was there was only the first of a search party.

She put her chin on her hands, and looked at the ground before her. Sparse grass, acorns, fallen branches. She felt a little sorry for Simon, now. For two reasons.

First, no matter how good his heart, Simon had gotten himself into what her grandmother would have called a pickle. If he didn't return to his own home, he would be a fugitive like herself.

She had decided what to do—to meet Eleanor and Spaulding behind the cattle barn the next night and, despite her broken heart, to leave the island.

But Simon couldn't do that. Well, of course, he could, but he wouldn't. While Merry herself loved the island and often thought of it as her own, the island really belonged more to the Mayhews.

One of Simon's great-great-great—she knew not how many—great-grandfathers had purchased the island from agents of the English king more than two hundred years earlier. More, Thomas Mayhew had settled the place, converted many of its Indians to Christ's lodge, and populated great tracts.

Everywhere one looked there was a Mayhew. The storekeeper; the owner of a gristmill—two current Mayhews owned gristmills; the family who ran the carding and fulling mill; sailing captains and chandlers and lobstermen and mapmakers and farmers and bankers and reverends.

Simon belonged to the Vineyard as much as the Vineyard belonged to his family.

She peeked over at Simon, who now had raised his head and was clearly trying to make out the sound of the carriage wheels passing. She smiled to herself. That was the second reason she felt badly for him just then: Simon was wild for carriages. Hiding here, in the woods, he could hardly stand not being able to peek out to identify the model and make and the family or tradesman who owned it.

To Merry, a carriage was a carriage. Perhaps a cart. To Simon, each vehicle had its pedigree. He studied drawings and pictures and catalogues endlessly. He knew that Ned Nickerson's grand brougham was made in Philadelphia before the War Between the States. He knew the various shades of upholstery a brougham might have, and from what mills and towns it came. He knew about different lamps hung to sit proudly at the shoulders of their drivers . . . even on Gerry Daggett's. He knew where Bernard Cleland was to stand and how much weight the perch would allow.

Simon knew the difference between the swift, lovely and sinuous lines of a cabriolet and the fleet, sleek chaise, even though to Merry they seemed quite alike. He could tell a Spring wagon from a simple dray at more than a quarter mile.

To have to lie low, head down and eyes averted, and not be able to exercise his greatest fancy was a genuine trial for Simon, Merry knew. If he fled the island with her, how many other, heavier and more sorrowful penalties would he have to pay?

twenty-six

In her rush to flee her home, to get to Eleanor's house and then to disappear again into the brush, Merry had remembered to bring clothing—her cape and Bailey's gown—and food. What she hadn't thought to bring was money. It was Simon who discovered this lapse. And it was Simon who decided that he would cut cross his uncle's farm and raid the larder in Frederick's house. If by chance he came upon anything that looked like a strongbox, or saw loose change lying about, just waiting for someone to collect it, he would do so.

Simon never doubted Merry's innocence, but just in case Mr. Fisher did not find the mystery visitor to the island within a certain period of time, Merry might well need supplies and shelter, more than she could trade for.

Merry sat quietly, almost shyly, under the trees and allowed Simon to do his thinking out loud. She watched his hands and face somberly, nodding from time to time, interrupting seldom. She wanted to do nothing that would give away the plan forming in her own mind.

For as soon as she was certain Simon was out of sight, heading towards the Mayhew farmhouse, Merry was going to stand and run. If she did not, Simon would be too deeply involved in what was, after all, her predicament, not his. It was one thing for the Skiffe family to bear the shame of a runaway; it was something else, more serious and more noteworthy, for the Mayhews to have lost a son to this sort of sad event.

" ~ I should be back within the hour, ~ " Simon continued.

Merry nodded that she understood.

" ~ You're to stay here, absolutely still, ~ " he insisted.
" ~ Don't move until I come back. Then we'll see where we can go for the night. ~ "

Merry agreed.

But she hadn't promised.

twenty-seven

Money was not something of which children on Martha's Vineyard had a great deal. It was something they rarely needed.

The neighborhood economies of the island rested solidly on a foundation of trading, swapping, a bucket of eels for a dozen eggs.

What one family had most of—eggs, tomatoes, fish, lamb—could always be traded for what they didn't have: linen, firewood, flour, lobsters.

There were stores throughout the up-island. In a pinch, Chilmark and Tisbury families would go to them and actually buy something they needed. But because so many of the items in these stores had to be imported, they were expensive. Their cost was increased not just by having to be transported across the Sound from New Bedford or the Cape or Plymouth, but also by whatever expense was involved in sending salesmen from those distant communities to walk the backroads of the island hawking their wares.

More often than not, if a family had run out of something they needed, someone would be sent first to Menemsha and then across the Sound to New Bedford to buy these items from the mainland stores, where prices were at least thirty per cent less.

In Merry's family, of course, it was Benjamin Skiffe who took these day trips to the mainland.

New Bedford as a town was not held high in the estimation of the islanders. The year-long odor of fish from its docks made them hold their noses as they talked about having to cross the water to go there. More, there were unsavory characters on that side of the water. Molly always reminded Ben Skiffe to fill his back pants pockets, where he kept his small amount of actual cash, with fishhooks, to thwart the pickpockets and thieves who thought Islanders were easy targets.

Merry sat motionlessly. Simon was nearly out of sight. In preparation, she brought her feet up under her, ready to stand and bolt.

She would have to stay well below the road between Edgartown and Tisbury. Because she couldn't hear the carriages on their busy ways to and from each township, she would have to stay out of sight, hidden. She would have to run from shelter to shelter, from wall to wall.

She had decided that it made sense to move in the direction of the fairgrounds in West Tisbury. She had, after all, only to pass one night alone in hiding before stationing herself behind the cattle sheds there, waiting to catch sight of Eleanor or Spaulding. It would be a long, difficult day, tomorrow, trying to stay unnoticed and yet finding a spot from which she could scan the sheds, the exhibition ring, and the grange itself until she saw her friends.

Merry counted to one hundred after Simon had dropped from sight. Then she jumped to her feet and without a glance back, began to run.

twenty-eight

Merry felt faint. She had last eaten before her fateful nap on the Vincent property. Now, in late afternoon, she began to regret that she hadn't been clever enough to wait for Simon's return. She could have eaten whatever he brought, pocketed what might have remained, and then—if only she had been so bright—then she might have persuaded Simon to return to his own family so that she alone might hide undetected until the time to meet Eleanor arrived.

She had stayed well below the Takemmy Trail. She had opened, it seemed to her, a hundred gates leading from pasture to field to pasture. Occasionally she had looked ahead and caught sight of someone tending flocks of sheep, or of someone else beginning to push a herd of cattle down towards a distant barn where they might be milked and brushed. At those moments, she had simply thrown herself facedown in the grass and waited until her path of flight was once more clear.

Her long cotton dress had been caught and pulled by the briers and thistles through which she had run. Idly she wished she had thought to wear her apron, too. It might have offered some protection from the thorns and sharp short fingers of fledgling scrub. Better, she could have used it to cover herself later, for the afternoon was wearing on, and the light above her was turning pale.

Looking ahead, Merry could hardly believe her good fortune. She could see a bridge, which must mean there was water below it. Oh, how thirsty she was now!

She did not run wildly towards her goal. Rather, she stopped, dropped to her knees, and sat in total stillness for a moment, squinting into the distance carefully.

She saw the bridge, and she thought, just beyond, the dark frame of a gristmill.

It was late in the season for grain or corn to be milled. Flour and meal should long ago have been bagged and tied and carted away. Still, there was just the small chance that some local farmer, someone whom she did not know, might still be inside working. She would have to approach with care.

Merry stayed low, almost crawling through the sparse grass, cut short by the grinding of sheeps' molars. There were few trees behind which she might hide quickly if she needed. She could begin now to smell the clear water ahead.

She was just about to run the few steps towards the stream's edge when, ahead of her, she saw something leap from the field and disappear again. She froze. She squinted across the distance and held her breath.

There! It happened a second time.

She smiled at her fears. What she had seen was a collie, herding the stragglers of a flock away and down towards a sheep cote she could not see. Ahead of the dog, perhaps another fifty feet or so, was the moving black broad-brimmed hat of a farmer. Every so often she saw the man raise his arm, and saw in his hand the light whip used to startle lazy ewes that insisted on dawdling over a final clump of sparse grass.

Merry was only a few feet from the rushing waters that eventually led to the wheel of the gristmill ahead. She was patient.

Daylight was fainter still by the time she felt secure enough to crawl forward and to lie sprawled on the bank of the stream. Daintily she dipped her cupped hands into the water and brought them to her lips. Oh, that was so good! So cool and sharp!

After a few more moments, she sat up. Twilight surrounded her. She could not think that men might still be at work in the mill. By now they would have finished—if, indeed, milling were still being done—and returned to their hearthsides.

She could see from her vantage the mill itself, sitting squatly on stone, its walls clapboarded and covered with vine. Its waterwheel moved ever so slowly, but only back and forth, not in a full rotation that would provide the power for the stone inside to make a full grinding turn.

Cautiously she rose and started forward. On the other side of the building, the side she could not see as she approached, there must be an entrance. And while inside there might be a rat or two still hungrily gnawing fallen kernels, Merry comforted herself with the idea that they would be satisfied enough with their meal of leavings not to look at her as dessert.

twenty-nine

The inside of the mill was darker than the evening outside. There was little need to put windows in a building such as this. It was a place of hard work and heavy dust. The one window there was seemed to hover above Merry, clouded by grain dust and, on its outer surface, rain-spotted. At the best of times, it couldn't have provided a lot of light. Rather it was there for ventilation.

Merry entered the square shell slowly. She squinted in what light there was, looking in corners and at floor level for the leavings of rodents. She found some. Well, at least she wasn't surprised. She stood absolutely still for a second and then, making as much noise as she could, she scurried from side to side, into each corner, around the fringe of the millage circle. If there were still rats around, she hoped they would be frightened enough to leave.

When she stopped, she couldn't help smiling. Silly fears; silly deeds. Still, she felt better as she examined the room, looking for the best place to sleep.

She hadn't a lot of choice. Every surface was flat and hard.

There was nothing in the mill that would give any worker even a moment's comfort. Rightly, she thought: people came here to work, not to rest.

The only wooden surface that wasn't cleared had grain leavings stacked on it. Someone, the mill's last user, had swept husks and grasses into a pile, no doubt to have been removed at the end of the day. Merry was grateful for the man's lapse.

At first she sat gingerly atop the pile of debris. She scrunched her bottom around. Well, it could have been worse. She leaned back against the wall.

She would not undress, or even take off her shoes. If there were rats about, why give them anything to nibble? She half-turned where she sat and pushed some of the grain remains towards the wall itself, to make a mound that might act as a support or even a pillow.

Leaning back slowly to test her handiwork, Merry smiled. It wasn't comfortable, but it also wasn't miserable. After all, it was warmer inside the mill than it would be out-of-doors. She was hidden from sight. And if by chance a storm blew up during the night, she would be dry.

She looked up at the dirty windowpane above her head. The glass was too clouded to see through, really, but early moonlight struggled to break into the space below. She was grateful for its effort.

Suddenly, she wished she could have seen a star, though. She needed to wish upon it.

She pushed her worry aside. She had only to get through one more day before meeting Eleanor and Spaulding. True enough, the alarm would have been raised. People in Chilmark and Tisbury itself would have been told about her flight. Yet there was a chance, the very smallest one, she admitted, but it was still there: suppose the mystery man, the man who now was remembered by the men who had met to gossip and joke at the store the Saturday night before, were spotted first.

A terrifying thought came then to her: suppose instead that the man hovered still about the scene of his crime. Suppose that night he chanced to take shelter in the very same place she did!

She shook her head, trying to calm herself. It was unthinkable that someone who had committed such horrors would still be on the island.

She fought her imaginary fear. There was more than enough that was real to keep her awake. For while she hadn't been able to hear the gasps of her neighbors as she had hurled the killing stone into the dust at her feet, she knew that the violence of her act had condemned her in many minds. A rich man had been murdered. It was important that someone be blamed.

Merry closed her eyes against all this.

A moment later she opened them once more to look at the smeared glass. She settled more comfortably into her nest, as comfortably as she could. She would concentrate on Eleanor and Spaulding and on her flight.

Eleanor's image floated in Merry's imagination. In one way, she felt badly about her cousin. Eleanor had never been strong physically. But it was exactly this that gave Merry hope now. If Eleanor had returned to Hartford on time, Merry would have no way to run, even if where she was running was unknown.

And if Eleanor hadn't been sickly, Merry herself might not have had the courage to spend a night alone in the gristmill.

Merry closed her eyes and smiled at her own memories. She had to admit that, for a time, she had been miserable, frightened and abandoned. Just a little more than a year ago to this very day, what had seemed at first so terrifying—living in the unknown—had softened into a chance to learn, to make new friends . . . really, to choose.

thirty

Molly Skiffe had held Merry's hand all the way cross the Sound, from Menemsha to New Bedford. While she knew the ache Ben would have in his heart until the following summer, Merry's mother had worked diligently to apply for Merry to be sent to the Asylum in Hartford.

The boat in which they sailed was not large. It carried bluefish, barley and potter's clay as well as its captain, his mate, and two boys of not more than fifteen who were along simply to give the other two the benefit of stronger, younger bodies at lifting and loading.

The fare on one of the three steamers that sailed between Cottage City or Vineyard Haven, and New Bedford, was one dollar. It would have cost Molly a return fare (two dollars) to escort Merry (three dollars) across to land. By offering fifty cents to the captain of the well-loaded little craft for the privilege of standing the entire crossing, the difference—a dollar and a half all tolled—was given to Merry to keep as money for an emergency. She also had instructions that that which she did not spend should be returned to the Skiffe family treasury.

Molly had known, when she fell in love with Benjamin, that should they have children, God willing, there was a chance one or more of them might be deaf. In the heat of her affection for Ben, though, this event seemed too distant to consider during their courtship, or even in the early days of their marriage.

Her parents had not been entirely approving of Molly's choice. Not because Benjamin was deaf, but because it was clear to them that the Skiffe family had seen better days and that there was little prospect of Ben's being able to return the family fortunes to what they had once been.

In the matter of Ben's hearing, Well, Molly's parents reasoned, this could happen to anyone. No one on the island considered this a handicap nor even a judgment from Above. Ben's sister and his two brothers were hearing. Some people heard; some didn't. They had no way of knowing how much more frequently families on the Vineyard, in particular in Chilmark and Tisbury, suffered deafness to appear amid the offspring of otherwise blossoming, comfortable homes.

As for the Skiffes, the family was an old and good one, reaching back nearly to the very time the island had been settled. The economy, and some poor choices, had over two hundred years brought the Skiffes to a level of subsistence rather than prosperity.

Because of her love for her younger daughter, Molly had delayed sending Merry off-island. She knew of the work at the Asylum; she knew that the state of Massachusetts, applied to properly, would pay Merry's tuition. And she'd had no difficulty, when finally she decided it was necessary, getting the Asylum's required recommendations and signatures from two respectable selectmen of Chilmark.

Merry herself had not wanted to leave the Vineyard. Molly had had to persuade her, to talk about the exciting world on the other side of the water, the opportunity to meet so many different kinds of people. As for schooling itself, Merry had always been a good performer in the schoolhouses on the island—scattered one-room structures students attended according to the season and their chores.

While Molly did not feel guilty having given birth to someone whose abilities were not as full as others, she did feel an extra responsibility. Ben had argued with her, but just a bit. After all, schooling on the island had stood him in good stead, and he couldn't see that the world was changing so fast that Merry wouldn't benefit from the same studies. But he loved his wife desperately, and to cause rupture or sorrow was something he would never do.

He never told Molly, though, how much he missed Merry.

Besides, with Ezra and Bailey and the ever rambunctious Pickup still on hand, both Ben and Molly knew that while there might be a gap in their family's attentions, there were others who demanded, and received, their share of love and cosseting.

Merry's trunk had been sent on ahead of her arrival in Hartford. The Asylum instructed that each child be well clothed, both for summers and winter. Each article was to be inventoried and marked with its owner's name. Ben had taken five dollars from the family's savings and forwarded that, too, by mail to the Asylum, as it suggested, for whatever expenses Merry might incur that were not covered by tuition.

The trip to Hartford would have been easier had Eleanor not fallen ill again in late August of last year. Eleanor had been attending school there since she was eight years old. She knew what to expect and how to ease Merry's way into the community. She could answer questions; she could comfort; she could explain.

With Eleanor ill, however, and in a state of semiquarantine, Molly Skiffe had tried her best to answer Merry's nervous questions. And it was she who checked train schedules and the Asylum's instructions to make certain nothing had been overlooked.

Molly was grateful both for her daughter's friendship with her cousin and for Merry's glowing good health, as opposed to Eleanor's spells and fevers. More, she was heartened by Eleanor's example. While it was undeniable that she seemed to have grown rather grand in her ways and in her manners, Eleanor was nonetheless bright and able, quicker with figures and with her fingers than most young people her age in Chilmark.

Merry could both read and write, too, as the Asylum recommended. Molly had tutored her; so had Bailey, and her teachers in school on the island. Even Ezra would spare a few moments from the end of his exhausting day, smelling of the sea and fish as he did, to stop to see if Merry needed assistance with her homework.

There was not a doubt in Molly's mind that sending Merry away was in her daughter's best interests, and she studied nightly the plan of study the Asylum offered, its rules and regulations, its proposals that would lead to self-sufficiency for its students.

The trip from Chilmark to Menemsha, to New Bedford, then via the Old Colony Railroad to Providence to catch a train to Hartford took a good part of the day. Merry and her mother had left their home before dawn. They were at the station in Providence just after two.

Once there, standing on the platform in a circle of sunshine on a breezy early autumn day, Molly completed her list of things to do. She handed Merry her extra money for emergencies. Merry was already carrying a basket of food and a cloak.

She gave Merry an envelope, sealed, which answered as the Asylum required the following questions: Merry's name in full (Merry Elizabeth Skiffe); her address; day, month, and year of her birth. Question four addressed the cause of Merry's deafness. Molly had written the only answer of which she could be certain: birth.

The four final questions seemed routine—names of parents; names of other children in the order of their age; were Merry's parents related before marriage? (not as far as was known, Molly wrote); did Merry have deaf-mute relatives? Here Molly had scowled to think and recall. Benjamin, of course; one of his parents; and one of her own, Molly's, aunts. Apart from Eleanor, Merry's cousin.

Finally, Molly handed her daughter a fresh, small leather-bound notebook and a pencil. This was to be used in case Merry found herself somewhere people did not speak sign language.

The locomotive of the Hartford, Providence and Fishkill line puffed importantly, impatient to begin chugging westwards. Molly sought out the conductor, assured herself that the man was staying aboard all the way through to Hartford, and entrusted her daughter to him. She offered him Merry's ticket, the cost of which, from Providence to Hartford alone, was $2.80. She bid her daughter farewell, swallowing her own tears, and turned away to begin her return journey to the island, destined to arrive back in Chilmark at dark.

The journey to Hartford was not a long one. The distance was barely ninety miles. Merry took a window seat and sat marveling at the landscape through which she rode. She opened her basket of provisions and ate daintily, carefully repacking it when she was finished with used linen and what she hadn't eaten.

She did not feel frightened, but she was definitely nervous. She understood why she was on the train, and what her parents hoped for from her experiences in Hartford. She would do her best. But at eleven years of age, she was still apprehensive.

Yes, she could run faster and farther than Simon Mayhew, her friend from school. And yes, again, she read almost as well as Eleanor, who was two years older than she. But she still felt like a tiny boat at the mercy of the enormous sea. She could not imagine from which direction a storm might arise, or how violent its wind and waves. And while she was proud of making this journey unaccompanied, deep down she longed for Eleanor at her side.

Hartford's depot was enormous to Merry, full of bustle and scurry. The conductor handed her down onto the platform gently and then, kindly, stood waiting with her for someone from the Asylum to arrive. Together they were islands in a busy sealane.

A half hour passed, and then another. Finally, eager to get to his own home and family and aware of darkness approaching, the conductor took Merry's hand and together they stepped out onto the walkway that faced the busy city. Merry's eyes grew large to see the enormity of the place, its many buildings and crowded streets. Horse-drawn cars carried citizens up and down the capitol hill; carriages and cabriolets flashed past. Vendors approached with fruit, flowers, shoelaces, food, newspapers. The conductor gently declined these treats as he nudged Merry towards a line of standing cabs.

She had no idea what the man shouted up at the cab's

driver, seated so high above the ground to drive his coach. The conductor took money from his own pocket and handed it up.

Turning then towards her, the conductor motioned that he needed Merry's notebook. She handed it to him, along with the pencil, but he took another from his own pocket and began writing.

"This kind man will deliver you to the Asylum. I have paid the fare. I wish you good fortune and an abiding trust in God."

Merry read this slowly when the notebook was handed to her. She looked up beseechingly at the conductor, not in fear but in a search for something to say or to give him that would tell him how thankful she was.

The man understood her look and, kindly, shook his head. Then he opened the cab's door and helped her mount the step to its inside. He stood waving on the pavement as the cab drove away from the station.

There was too much newness all around for Merry to take in. She knew she should be trying to remember everything she saw so that she could include it in her first letter home. But she lost count of the sights she had never before seen, or even imagined, and before she had time to prepare, she was being driven up a gravelled drive towards the biggest building she had ever seen in her life.

Situated at the top of Asylum Avenue, the American Asylum for the Deaf and Dumb was a graceful four-storied edifice. The gravel drive on which Merry's cab drove passed one half of the building's enormous facade before stopping below eight wooden steps that led upwards to a porch and the main entryway.

Merry was helped down from the coach, patted once on the shoulder and smiled at, and then left alone on the drive.

She looked forlornly after the coachman and then turned to stare.

The building itself was wood. It had two huge wings attached to its central core. Its front was imposing and ornate. There were nine balconies in all, in two stories, where students and teachers might gather to look down upon the front lawn. Merry imagined herself up under the curved beams, leaning against one of the white-painted stencils that formed its barriers. She dutifully turned, as she would have from her imaginary perch, to look at the acres of trees and grass, all maintained beautifully and neatly.

As she stood facing away from the school itself, aware of the fading light and just the tiniest bit frightened, a hand came to rest lightly on her shoulder. Merry was startled but tried not to show it. She turned to look into the face of a woman whose age was impossible to determine, dressed in dark, long clothing, and wearing eyeglasses. The woman's hair was parted in the middle and gathered in a bun, gray and dark brown mixed. Her eyes, behind her lens, seemed very, very alert but also somehow gentle.

Remembering her mother's instructions, Merry curtsied. The older woman smiled and bowed, just a little, before straightening up to address Merry.

But Merry couldn't grasp all that the woman was saying. Her eyes followed the woman's hands and Merry understood that there was a question implied, and repeated. Merry stood on the drive and put down her basket. She reached into a pocket of her cape and brought out the letter her mother had given her in Providence. She handed it up to the woman.

After a moment of reading, the woman looked down at Merry and smiled. She said something more. Merry thought it might have to do with a book. What book?

117

Then she remembered the notebook her mother had given her. She pulled that out, too, and handed it up to the woman, waiting patiently as a pencil on a silver chain was drawn down from a pin on the breast of this woman.

Merry took back the notebook to read, "Miss Skiffe, you have arrived here a day early."

By that very first night, Merry had understood many things.

The woman—Miss Sarah Beach, the mistress of the tailor shop—had explained that the Asylum opened every year on the same day, the second Wednesday of September. Merry was the first and only student to arrive. Preparations for the school year were not yet complete. The kitchen staff, for example, was not expected in full force until the following day.

Using Merry's notebook, as well as her hands, Miss Beach guessed that perhaps life on Martha's Vineyard was unlike that of the city, and that it must be easy to grow confused about time when one worked as hard and unstintingly as one must to keep alive. Merry accepted the explanation with a sinking feeling in her heart.

Her mother's love and good intentions aside, how many other things had Molly gleaned from her reading that might not now turn out to be so?

Even as Miss Beach led Merry into the girls' dormitory, Merry was beset by a terrible fear: she had never before been in this part of the world. How was she even sure she had arrived where she was expected? How could she be certain this place really was a school at all? With no other young people to be seen, Merry's imagination took flame: she might very well be in danger.

The evidence before her eyes calmed her somewhat. Miss

Beach led her into a long room with a high ceiling. Two rows of neatly made-up beds ran lengthwise down its center, each with an attendant straight chair beside it. Other beds and chairs surrounded these neatly aligned single beds. There were eight standing poles made of painted steel that ran from the shined wooden floor to the ceiling that seemed to separate the dormitory's aisles. Merry couldn't imagine what they were for.

Miss Beach left Merry standing at the top of the room for a moment as she walked between the beds and chairs, bending down to look under each bed at the names on the trunks resting there. Finally she stopped and signalled Merry to come. Merry walked forwards and found her very own trunk under a bed that sat pristinely between two tall windows.

She was enormously relieved.

Merry did not eat supper that evening in the Asylum's dining hall. Rather, Miss Beach accompanied her to the kitchen and there, between the two of them, they selected bread and cheese, fruit and milk, from the gigantic larder that was stocked to its ceiling with provisions for the school year that would begin the following day.

Merry had begun to better understand the signs Miss Beach used to communicate. Actually, the more time spent between them, the clearer Merry saw that some of the signs were not so very strange, were really quite like some she was accustomed to using on the Vineyard.

For her part, Miss Beach explained carefully that the signs Merry had used all her life were probably centuries old and not even native to American sign language as it had then developed. She spoke of other girls from the Vineyard, Eleanor included, who arrived experiencing the same confusion. But really, she added finally, if one thought a bit, one should be proud of coming from the Vineyard, since the signs in use there trailed back across the Atlantic to the villages and hamlets of England itself.

In bed that night, in her nightgown, her own robe folded neatly at the foot of her bed, despite the gentle words of Miss Beach, Merry felt abandoned and concerned. If she had stumbled so badly in understanding the thoughtful Miss Beach, however could she expect to understand other teachers, not to mention her classmates?

In the moonlight that streamed into the huge unadorned room, Merry looked around and could hardly believe that so many girls would arrive next morning to fill so many beds. Putting Eleanor aside, for who knew when she might be well enough to travel, would there be someone else to help ease her into this new experience?

Would coming from Chilmark brand her as being so different people would remark on it? If she had trouble grasping what was said to her by such a kind woman as Miss Beach, would her classmates have the same difficulty understanding what she, Merry, said?

The idea that she might have to live for eight months in confusion and solitude almost brought Merry to tears.

Almost. Then she counselled herself: her family had expectations. Her family trusted her, had hopes for her, loved her. She would not cry. She would not disappoint them.

This determination forced her to settle back into her pillow, her hands resting lightly atop her coverlet, no longer fearful.

And so she slept.

thirty-one

In the mill, Merry had gone to sleep so early that she awoke while it was still dark. Immediately she was hungry. She stood and brushed from her clothing the awns and leavings in which she had lain during the night. She pushed open the door to the outside slowly and carefully but fairly certain nothing threatening awaited her.

She rushed to the bank of the stream that powered the mill, knelt carefully there since the dew was still damp upon the grass, and put her hands in its water. It was cool, colder than the day before, but she drank eagerly from it and dipped her hands in again to wash her face and neck.

She leaned back on her knees to think. It was still too dark to begin to pick berries as she ran towards the fairgrounds; a mistake could prove dangerous. There were lovely plants on the island whose fruit was not.

Still, she had to be underway soon. She wanted to reach the trees that grew behind the cattle sheds at the fairgrounds early enough to find a good spot to hide, a place from which she could look out over the fair and later, oh how she hoped! where she would see Eleanor and Spaulding.

She leaned forward to retie her hightop shoes. Then she stood to brush off her long shirt. She shivered. Autumn was finally working its way cross the Sound towards the island. Within weeks there might even be ice on some of the freshwater ponds that dotted the fields and forests.

She turned then to begin her trek cross country. She stopped in her tracks. There, not more than twenty feet ahead of her, were a whitetail doe and her fawn, also frozen in time. They seemed to have waited patiently for her to drink and neaten and to then move away so they could take their turn at the stream.

It was still dark, but Merry wished she had her notebook at hand. She would have loved to draw them both, stockstill, eager but controlled, sweetly waiting together to drink. Miss Beach would so enjoy the picture.

Merry moved slowly, cautious not to startle the deer. A few paces away from them, she turned finally and began walking quickly through the underbrush. Idly she wondered whether deer ever were born deaf.

thirty-two

Merry made fairly good progress before the sun rose over the horizon. The ground before her, the mile and a half between where she had slept and the fairgrounds, was largely flat. Huge boulders too heavy to be moved, too large even to be used in stone walls, sat in pastures as they had for centuries, offering thin shelter and shade to the herds of sheep that would graze around them.

The Tiasquam River, which powered the gristmill, idled first towards the northeast and then, far ahead of where she walked now, took a turn south towards the shore, meeting Long Cove that ran down to the sea. In fact, if she followed the water, alternately narrow and then broadening into ponds along its course, she would have been able to see across the cove towards where she had sheltered not so very long ago, at the bottom of Lucy and Bedford Vincent's farm.

Hunger drove Merry now, as much as the need to arrive at a safe vantage behind the cattle barns. There were dozens of plants along her trail that offered to passersby the prospect of sweet relief. But Merry also knew that danger could lie in stripping berries from every branch and eating them.

The brightly colored red leaves of the autumn Virginia creeper surrounded lovely little dark blue berries, much like blueberries themselves. But they were poison. So, too, were the open berries of the bittersweet; birds could sweep down to eat, but for all others, illness quickly followed.

Even black cherry trees offered trouble. The cherries themselves were slightly sour but they could be used to make a fine jelly or jam. Their pits, however, had to be removed before boiling, or thrown away if one ate them, because they were toxic.

The few bushes Merry came to, standing alongside a gate or mixed in with scrub pine and oak, did not offer a feast. It was late in the season, and while there had been no frost yet, much of the fruit from the huckleberrys and blueberrys had dropped to the ground, or been eaten by blue jays and thrashers.

Merry was not far from the quiet water of one of the Tiasquam's ponds when she saw a sheepdog bound over the horizon. Immediately she dropped to the ground, hoping against hope the dog had neither seen nor scented her. The day's breeze was from the north, from the mainland, so in all likelihood the dog was romping ahead of its flock in high spirits, only stretching out muscles that might have tightened during the night. The real question was whether the dog was being followed by its master, or was experienced enough to run the flock itself, responding to calls and whistles from far off.

She lay facedown, holding her breath. Behind her squeezed-shut eyes she recalled the landscape just ahead. At the water's edge was a stand of trees. They could hide her.

Better, they might have wild grapevines wrapped around and over their lower limbs. If only she could get there.

She raised her head. She was too low to the ground to catch sight of the dog. She would have to stand. But she didn't want to: if the dog were in a nearby field, it would come running, barking, alerting anyone in the area to its human discovery.

Merry began to crawl towards the water, slowly, creeping a few feet at a time and then stopping. She could not hear, of course, whether the dog had seen her, whether he might even now be bearing down upon her. She could only pray.

She continued painstakingly towards the pond, her heart in her throat. Even if she had been able to hear, the rustle of her clothes on the ground, the little puffs of air she exhaled to keep flying bugs from her mouth and eyes, combined with her heart's drumlike rhythmic pulse would have covered the sound of the careful footsteps behind her.

thirty-three

Safe in the clump of trees, Merry rose to her knees, slowly. She looked in the direction in which she had seen the gamboling dog. He was nowhere to be seen.

Sighing, Merry smiled. She scooted a few feet more towards the water and dipped her hand into it. She brought what she could to her mouth four or five times. She wiped her hand on her dress and pulled up again, onto her knees.

As though provided from Above, a wild grape wound its tendrils around a young gray birch. She reached up and plucked a handful of the fruit that remained. Oh, it was delicious! She closed her eyes to savor the taste, to memorize it.

At that moment, a hand descended. It touched Merry's shoulder.

White-faced and heart-stopped, Merry turned fast, ready to bolt.

Jared Snipes grinned down at her.

Merry nearly collapsed with relief before she remembered that, even though he was an Indian, Jared might have been hunting her down for Mr. Fisher. She stared at him, waiting for she dared not think what.

Jared Snipes smiled still and then hunkered down beside Merry. His black hair was cut neatly, his breeches made of wool. He wore a deerskin jacket atop his ordinary work shirt. On his shoulder, from a strap, hung a small leather bag.

The two stared at each other a moment more.

" ~ Don't you remember me? ~ "

Merry nodded.

Jared made a false face of sorrow. " ~ Aren't we still friends? ~ "

~ Of course we are. ~

" ~ Then why are you so fearful? ~ "

Merry did not at first know what to reply. If Jared hadn't heard about the trial, for that was how she regarded the appointment at noon the day before, he must have heard about Ned Nickerson's murder. If he had heard about the trial, then surely he must also know she was a fugitive now.

Before she could decide to say anything at all, Jared put a finger to his lips. He pointed with his other hand.

Merry followed his direction.

Not fifty feet away two heath hens strolled through sparse grasses, pecking at this seed or that insect.

Heath hens prospered on the cleared pastureland of the Vineyard. It was not unusual to see them. Or, at least, it had not been unusual until lately. With hawks above diving, owls at night swooping, foxes and raccoons stalking, their numbers were dwindling. Although in open country they flourished and grew fat—rounder than a grouse and rather larger, with shorter, stubbier white and brown tails—the very flatness of their surroundings gave them little cover.

Besides, roasted heath hen was wonderful to taste.

~ Oh, how I wish we had a fire! ~ Merry ached.

" ~ If you could catch them, ~ " Jared Snipes reminded her.

~ I could, I know I could. Oh, I am so hungry! ~

" ~ But what are you doing here, so far from your farm? ~ "

He *didn't* know! He hadn't been following her for Mr. Fisher! Without thinking, Merry leaned up on her knees and reached to hug Jared's shoulders.

When she sat back, Jared asked his question again.

Hard as she tried not to, Merry blushed. ~ I wanted to get to the fair early. ~

" ~ Early? No one will be there at all ~ "

~ How far away do you think I am? ~

Jared considered. " ~ Perhaps an hour. The country is rough. I would take less time. Our strides differ. ~ "

Merry nodded reasonably. ~ But what are you doing out so early? ~

Jared smiled. " ~ It isn't early. I left last sundown. ~ "

~ Where are you going? ~

Jared grew more serious. " ~ To speak to my great-grand-father. ~ "

~ Where is he? ~

" ~ At Katama, ~ " Jared replied, making the signs for the country between Herring Creek and Chappaquiddick Island. " ~ He died there. ~ "

Merry nodded wisely. Indians often wandered the island on their own errands, on their own quests. She felt that to ask more would be impolite.

" ~ Would you like to eat with me? ~ " Jared asked then.

~ Oh yes, please! ~ Merry's face glowed.

Jared shrugged the small bag from his shoulder. He put it on the ground before him and began to pull from it his victuals: roasted, sliced, and then dried venison, apples and chunks of dried salt cod, bread. He handed Merry a piece of venison and she began to chew on it, squeezing from it the gamey but sweet flavors.

They sat together for a few moments eating in silence. Jared shared whatever Merry indicated she wanted to try. He was amused at how grateful she seemed to be.

After a while, Merry wiped her mouth with a corner of her long skirt. She felt better, stronger. ~ Do you know of Mr. Nickerson's death? ~ she asked only slightly timidly.

Jared nodded that he did. " ~ But it has nothing to do with us. ~ "

~ He was *murdered*. ~

Jared smiled reflectively. " ~ You read too much about Indians across the water, ~ " he said. " ~ We are Wampanoags, Algonquin. Not Apaches or Comanches. We are not savages. ~ "

~ Yes, I know, but— ~

Jared raised a hand to stop Merry. " ~ Remember, please, *we* are civilized. Long before Mr. Mayhew converted us we believed in the goodness of the world. He did not have to work hard. We also believed in peace. We do still. ~ "

Merry reddened, chastened. She looked down at the ground between them.

Jared reached out to touch Merry's shoulder. " ~ Would you care to walk my way? ~ " he asked.

Merry looked up, puzzled.

" ~ We walk in the same direction, Merry. ~ "

Merry thought a moment. She would love the company, and the food. And she was fond of Jared. But did she dare stand tall and pace beside him? Two people were more visible than one darting and dodging from public view. And she couldn't explain to Jared why she had to be so canny.

~ I'll rest here awhile, ~ she announced. ~ You go on. Your grandfather must be impatient. ~

Jared did not argue. He collected his goods and stuffed what was left back into his pack. He hitched the bag onto his shoulder and stood up. " ~ If you follow the water, the fair is only a few hundred paces from the last pond you see. ~ "

~ Thank you. I'll remember. And thank you for the food, Jared. ~

Seriously, Jared nodded. " ~ Perhaps, when I return, we shall meet again on the beach. I shall have oysters, and you—? ~ "

Merry grinned. ~ Saltmarsh hay. We can trade. ~

Jared Snipes raised his hand in farewell and strode off.

Merry would have been happier just then but she suddenly squinted to follow his receding figure. Out there, somewhere, was a sheepdog. She would try to see whether Jared drew its attention. If he did, she would leap to her feet and run.

As Jared's figure began to grow small in the distance, Merry scowled. Jared had mentioned the beach. Now, in her mind, Merry saw the strand, its rocks and boulders, the surf. What she didn't see was Bailey and herself trading with Jared as they had done not so very long ago. She saw instead the dark figure of Ned Nickerson.

thirty-four

Merry had not known that Edward Nickerson was riding towards her.

She was bent over her pad, intent on sketching the sea which swirled that cool, clouded afternoon around the remains of a dory that had washed to shore. Merry had not given thought to whose boat it must be, or to what had happened to its owner. She knew what could have happened—just so to her brother Ezra—but the boards and beam of the boat were bleached so white that she preferred to think it had slipped its mooring somewhere years before and taken its own voyage out to sea. It had lain now upon the beach some weeks, anyway, being pushed in and out by the tide.

Hoofbeats on the pebbles and rocks above the beach were inaudible to Merry. So, too, were the footsteps that began so suddenly with a crunch, as Mr. Nickerson jumped down from his horse on to the sand and approached her.

When Merry next raised her pen from the pad to look up

at the derelict boat, what she saw was Edward Nickerson standing directly in front of her, his legs spread wide apart, his arms crossed over his chest, an odd expression on his face. His dark hair was long and the wind from the ocean blew so hard that every once in a while it seemed to stand straight up from the back of his head.

"A young pretty thing like you here, unchaperoned?"

Merry could not hear the deep tones of Nickerson's voice. She told him so.

" ~ Are you alone here, miss? Unchaperoned? ~ "

Merry nodded. Why should she not be?

With no warning then, Nickerson took a huge step towards her and knelt directly in front of her, staring into her face. Merry was startled, and beginning to be uneasy. She stared back into his dark eyes, waiting.

" ~ You are charming-looking. Has anyone commented? ~ "

Merry shook her head truthfully.

Edward Nickerson smiled encouragingly. " ~ Well, ~ " he said, " ~ it's quite true, you know. You have lovely eyes. ~ "

Merry waited, her breathing now somewhat shorter.

Nickerson reached out quickly and grabbed for Merry's free hand. Confidently he pulled her to her feet, so quickly that both her pen and her drawing book fell from her grasp.

" ~ You could be well rewarded, you know. ~ "

~ For what? ~

" ~ For attending to me at my home, ~ " Nickerson replied. " ~ Your duties would be light and I could supervise your schooling. In fact, I could teach you myself, right there. You wouldn't have to go to school ever again. ~ "

Merry was now frightened of this man. She stepped back quickly but Nickerson reached out again for her hand, clasping it more tightly than before.

Despite her fear, Merry looked directly into the man's eyes

132

and held his glance. She wanted to tell him something. With a huge effort, she broke his grip.

~ I can call out, you know. ~

Nickerson laughed. " ~ Who is to hear? The sea? ~ "

Merry next thought of running, but the sight of Nickerson's strong horse, at least sixteen hands high, put an end to this plan. She was beginning to get angry.

~ I should be of no use to you. ~

" ~ You have no way of knowing. ~ "

~ A serving girl with no hands could do no work. ~

" ~ No hands? ~ "

Merry nodded vigorously. ~ To keep me, you would have to silence me. You would have to sever my hands from my arms. ~ She was defiant now. ~ I also know how to write. ~

Nickerson stared at her a moment and then once more reached out like a snake. The look in his eyes was clear.

Merry spun, hoping to take him by surprise. She took two quick steps on the sand.

Nickerson laughed as he hauled her in again.

Merry looked up into his face and then, not knowing what would emerge, she closed her eyes and opened her mouth.

Nickerson dropped her hand as though it were on fire.

Merry opened her eyes. She saw Nickerson's face, paled, frightened. She had a weapon! She closed her eyes again against whatever sound she was going to produce, and opened her mouth wide.

Once more she looked at Nickerson. He had not moved. " ~ How old *are* you? ~ " he demanded, looking still astonished.

Merry did not even try to reply. Instead, she knelt quickly, gathered her notebook and pen, and started to race away, up the beach towards the flatlands that gave onto the sea.

At the top of a dune, she looked over her shoulder, certain she would see Nickerson's steed charging down upon her.

But Nickerson was just then mounting. He did not look up at her. He spurred his horse's flanks and began to gallop towards the west.

Merry watched a moment more before understanding she was free.

Then she sat hard upon the earth and began to shake.

thirty-five

Merry's reveries ended. Goodness! Jared Snipes had long ago disappeared over the horizon.

The sun was now nearly directly above her head. She stood slowly, carefully scanning the distance for signs of man or animal.

Jared had advised her to follow the stream. She looked at the thread of shining water that now led slightly to the north. There were trees all along its banks, good cover. She would follow his suggestion.

She started out slowly, breaking her way through weed and fall flower, trying to be careful not to break branches or to leave footprints. She avoided puddles and mud. Occasionally she had to bend down, gather leaves and sticks in her arms, throw them ahead of her, and then, finally, step gingerly across a patch of ground where footprints would have signalled to a search party that they were not far from their prey.

Merry was not in a rush. Security was what mattered most to her, being invisible. Besides, Jared had told her that the fairgrounds really were not all that far from where they had shared his food. What was she going to do when she finally arrived at her destination? There was nothing in her future but hiding until the appointed hour.

It was not long before Merry came to a tall stone marker, a post that was so new vines had only begun to climb its base. This was but one of many that ran down a line from Cedar Tree Neck in the north to the top of Tisbury Great Pond, which marked the boundaries between the towns of Chilmark and West Tisbury. The island fairgrounds were located in West Tisbury.

Merry passed the sentry stone with a sense that a major decision was being made in her life.

As she made her slow way eastwards, she could see an increasing number of stands of pine and oak, uncut, untouched. The ground was flat and fit for little but sheep or cattle, but these clumps of color and shade on the horizon gave her confidence. She knew she was still well below Middle Road, along which any number of people might be pursuing her. She smiled at her own thought. If she had to, she could run and dart from sentinel to sentry post.

Another small pond lay directly in her path. She drank from it and then stood thoughtfully. She could not be that far from her goal. Before her, the Tiasquam now turned south towards the sea. Surely Jared couldn't have meant for her to follow the river that far? She knew the fairgrounds were near the center of the island.

She closed her eyes against the sun and tried to picture her goal. She could not recall seeing water near the fairgrounds. Behind the cattle barns, where she was going to hide, there was a thin stand of trees that marked the separation of the township property from someone's farm. It was a weather break in addition to a property line. But was there water nearby?

Merry opened her eyes, her decision made. Jared had been kind to her, always. She would take his advice. She would continue on the path he directed. If the stream really did run past the fairgrounds, surely she would see carriages or flags or the top of the grange building itself.

Eager suddenly to be where she would feel safe once more, Merry walked faster. She stopped only once, to let a dazed-looking bushy-tailed young red fox cross her path. After it had disappeared into the brush, Merry finally crossed the Tiasquam cautiously, running atop moss-covered rocks that seemed to invite travellers to use them thus.

Faster than she would have thought, Merry came to another pond, this one larger than the last. She edged around its northeast side, not certain once again how far to go.

Puzzlement did not last. Looking around to see whether she were being observed, she caught sight of the top of the grange itself, up a slight hill, just barely visible through the trees in which she planned to hide. It couldn't have been more than two or three hundred yards away.

Between where Merry stood and the trees that would hide her was only a field with a flock of thirty or forty sheep grazing. To the north was the farmhouse to which the animals belonged. She saw neither tending dog nor shepherd.

Feeling as though what energy she had left would barely last until she were safe in the trees, and hoping against hope that no one appeared to give the alarm, Merry began to run recklessly up the slight hill.

thirty-six

Spaulding Mayhew saw Merry's mad dash for cover. He had been watching for her.

Taller than his cousin Simon by at least a head, and of a fuller, more rounded masculine shape, Spaulding had ridden one of his father's coach horses Indian style to the fairgrounds as soon as his own chores were completed. The late morning air had seemed to him somehow—despite the open crisp thinness through which he rode—ominous. Colors in the bushes and trees he passed seemed too bright. Sounds were unnaturally clear. He felt the mount beneath him quiver and shy. He had been astonished to see his own hands shake these past few days. Together, they were a nervous pair.

He tied up the roan with other horses behind the cattle sheds, and had stood as coolly as he could, fiddling uncomfortably with the tack of the horse's bridle.

Sometimes he would be called to. Every new voice nearly made him stammer with fear and nerves. Still, he managed to answer politely each inquiry about his health, his family's, his plans for the fair. But every few seconds he looked over his shoulder, waiting for Merry to arrive.

The sheds were open-sided, barely roofed structures that could contain livestock of any sort. Divided into cubicles, each partitioned stall had wood at its base, but at the height of one's waist they opened to the air. Pigs and sheep could be penned; cattle and horses stalled and fed. Rabbits and chickens were also kept in these sheds, but in wired cages atop wooden crates.

Between the sheds themselves and the grange hall was an open field in which stood a wooden ring. Citizens of Dukes County could thus stand around its railings to cheer or discuss what was being shown or offered. No sales were made at the fair itself, but a hawkeyed farmer could often spot a ewe or heifer he needed for his own herd. Afterwards, perhaps two or three days later, he would approach its owner and try to effect a trade. Failing this, he would part with some of his hard-earned and cannily hoarded Yankee cash.

The grange itself was a weathered gray wooden pile, its first story fatter than its second, a style called "hoop-skirted." Inside were displays of vegetables, preserved foods, handicrafts, drawings, flowers.

The building reminded Spaulding of pictures he had seen in books of what Noah's ark may have looked like. Although it had a peaked roof, with wooden fringe ringing the eaves, and a stolid first floor, windowed, where there was more ginger-bread, the whole building looked like an unwieldy ship that could be pushed by a gale out onto the high seas.

The idea made Spaulding smile for the first time since

Eleanor had told him about the Skiffe visit. That would serve them right, he thought, all the people inside fingering displays and complimenting one another's summer industry. What a laugh: a giant wave swallowing the entire island, and the hall floating out to sea on its tide.

He nearly jumped from his boots as a goose waddled by, loose and free of its tether. Within a few seconds a small girl gave chase and the two disappeared behind the figures of other fairgoers. He breathed deeply and cautioned himself. Calm was everything. Appearance mattered. He must do nothing apart from what people expected.

Spaulding had been waiting for Merry since nearly noon. Along with other townspeople from Chilmark on their way to the fair, he had scoured the hillsides and fields through which he rode for signs of her. What only he and Eleanor knew before—what Merry's destination was, what her plans were—was now known by the entire Skiffe clan. And while he despised himself for having had the thought, there was one he could not shake: it was vital now that Merry flee the island with them. He had not thought it through when Eleanor first had told him of her cousin's need. It seemed only an inconvenience to be weighted down with such a child. But now her very body beside his own was a guarantee of freedom!

He shook his head, his longish brown hair whipping around his cheeks. He admired Bailey, for she was a beauty. But how she could weasel! And he had thought, he had believed, that Eleanor herself was stronger, more able to resist any reason, any question. Their lives together depended on this secret start, this flight from their families. Hadn't she realized that by telling the Skiffes where Merry might be, their own plans of beginning a new life together were in jeopardy?

Spaulding frowned: more was imperilled than a marriage.

He closed his eyes and shook his head to clear the image of a young man writhing at the end of a rope.

He hadn't meant for Nickerson to die.

Nor had he, Spaulding, intended to become a thief.

The idea that others were suspected of his accidental deed did not lighten his heart.

He laughed bitterly at himself. Lately it seemed to him that—no matter how carefully he planned—his entire life was uncharted, unintended, beyond what he could control.

What had happened had been so much spur of the moment that—Spaulding stopped his own thought. No, part of it was not. He had known Nickerson to be carousing with friends. He had known his route returning to Indian Hill. He had hidden carefully, gentling his horse just off the lane in shadows, waiting. He even knew in which pocket Nickerson's money was.

He had never liked Ned Nickerson. Not that that was a reason, an excuse. But it made him feel better about what he planned—the relief of Mr. Nickerson's heavy vest pocket, and the subsequent putting to good use of Mr. Nickerson's ill-gotten gains.

About his own role in getting those gains, Spaulding had argued long and thoughtfully with himself. He made more working a few hours on the odd Saturday night for Nickerson than he did on his coastal journeys as cook and cabin boy in others' ships. He knew others did Nickerson's bidding when he could not.

He always had alibis galore, insofar as he could slip off a ship at Edgartown and ride inland, or debark in Vineyard Haven and ride south. He could relieve a pen of whatever prize it held that Nickerson wanted, deliver it to Indian Hill, and be back on board cooking fish and potatoes on a little steerage stove in no time.

Spaulding was man enough not to try to excuse his deeds

as good ones. Still, if he hadn't rescued the lamb, the yearling, the heifer, who knew what would have become of them facing winter and little food and no care?

He knew he was enriching a man he did not like, a man no one else on the island liked or admired. But he had his reasons.

Eleanor.

Their future together.

All endangered by Nickerson's hold over him, by his threat to expose Spaulding—a child of comparative privilege on the island—as better than no one else, even Gerry Daggett or Bernard Cleland.

He shook his head again in thought. Although the idea might be blasphemous, God had assisted at every step.

Spaulding had never imagined that Nickerson would be facedown in the road, half-conscious and in pain, blood seeping around his collar.

Nickerson had blindly raised an arm, seeking aid or assistance from whomever stood nearby. For just the shortest second this had nearly stopped Spaulding. What he feared suddenly, there in the dark on a road where a carriage or trap might appear at any moment, was that Nickerson might look up to recognize him and then later, if Spaulding did give aid and comfort, identify him. Which, in itself, would have been nothing to fear but for the fact that Spaulding's intent was to relieve the man of the weight of bills and coin in his vest.

The large stone, newly fallen from a wall nearby or even perhaps having been dislodged as Nickerson fell from his steed, was providential, too. For there was no other way Spaulding could have followed through on his scheme. To have done something so shameful to a man still aware and conscious and able to cry out would have been too much for nearly any man.

Everything had happened so quickly, in such a panic of

speed and discovery and need, that even now, thinking about it, Spaulding was astonished by his own deed.

And not proud.

He thought again about how easily Eleanor had given up her information to Bailey Skiffe. He told himself he was probably being unfair. He could not know what pressure Bailey had used with Eleanor, or how much other influence was brought to bear by her own family.

He scraped the bottom of his boots along a rock. He had been taught not to judge others harshly.

He smiled at another thought: Eleanor said one of the reasons she doted on him was because he did not judge. Nothing he said or thought to her or of her was harsh or critical. How could it be otherwise? He loved her.

He wasn't as fond of Merry, though. He turned again and finally, at last, saw Merry's thin form cross the field behind the sheds and drop out of sight in tall grass, behind the stand of trees that separated the agricultural society's land from the farm behind.

He pulled out his pocket watch: nearly two.

He turned back to glance at the fair and its crowds. He would have liked to have spent time with them, walking thoughtfully through the grange aisles, admiring the hard work of his neighbors. One last time. Guiltless.

He would like to have forgotten Merry altogether and stayed where he was, moving to the rail of the ring to watch livestock being marched around, all combed and shined and in the hands of loving caretakers, some adult and some children—for there were classes at the fair, and prizes, too, for children. And he was keen to see what curiosities the new Dime Museum—for the first time brought over from the mainland especially for the fair—had to display for his ten cents.

Guiltless.

He could do none of that now. What he had first to do was warn Merry, hide her somewhere other than where her family expected. Then he had to spirit his beloved away from her family at the fair unseen.

And always, from the moment he clasped Eleanor's hand in his and rode for Vineyard Haven, from the next day's dawn when together they would board a steamer for New Bedford—for the next fifty years—he would have to carry his fatal secret alone.

Unless . . . unless . . . it was a thought that Spaulding rejected almost as quickly as it surfaced. He *could* flee alone. He could escape the island. He could find work. He could send for Eleanor later.

To do so was a confession. To do so was cowardice. To do so might well cause him to lose Eleanor altogether.

He put this possibility from his mind forever.

Only Spaulding knew that Merry had no need to run from justice. No case had been brought against her. There was, as yet, no real evidence, nor would there be any.

But his affection for Eleanor had been the cause of his heated ride to the fairgrounds. If she believed, and Spaulding could not doubt this, that her cousin was in mortal danger, then he had no choice. In his heart, he hoped that Merry's escape from the island would be only a temporary one. He knew for certain he didn't want her to travel with him and his new wife. Unworthy though the thought was, he also knew that if Merry did flee with them, she would be as good as admitting, if not guilt, then at least secret knowledge of Ned Nickerson's death.

What he really needed was time to plan. He and Eleanor now would be watched, trailed, remarked upon by everyone who knew what they had devised. (Why couldn't Eleanor just have told the Skiffes where Merry was likely to be instead of so proudly explaining why? That was Bailey's influence, he was certain.)

He pushed himself away from his horse and took a few steps towards the trees, glancing over his shoulder to see whether his movements were noted by his family's neighbors or friends. On a small island like the Vineyard, little in daylight could be done secretly.

It would not do to frighten Merry. Better to let her see him coming, to wonder why.

He remembered her brother Ezra, and his loss. He would try to be as patient as Ezra had always been with Merry.

That would not be easy. Merry was a determined little thing, too ready to argue. Not at all like Eleanor who agreed always with Spaulding's visions of life, as a woman should.

thirty-seven

Merry sat in the sparse grasses that grew between trees and looked down at herself. Her dress was ruined, there was no doubt. Stained, torn, dirty beyond washing. What a picture she would make boarding the ferry.

If only Ezra had lived.

It was the sea itself that was changing Merry's life. Not old Ned Nickerson.

If Ezra had been alive, he would have advised her, perhaps even fled with her to the mainland. He would have cared for her, seen to it that she was sheltered and fed and safely out of reach of the constable, Mr. Fisher.

Merry raised a hand to shield her eyes as she looked upwards at the sun. There was still *so* much time. She ached to be gone now, to be with Eleanor and Spaulding, racing through the night fog towards a new and happier life.

She felt tears form in her eyes. She cautioned herself against self-pity. It was not only unbecoming, it was not the path to solving one's problems.

Actually, she thought now, bringing her hand down and snuggling into her ground-level nest, despite the way she looked she had not done badly so far. Ezra would have been proud of her industry, her independence.

It was Ezra who had given her hope a year ago, when she had brought her drawings—on single sheets of cast-off paper—to the fair to be entered in the young people's drawing competition. She and Ezra had walked slowly through the grange and stood studying others' colorful work. " ~ They're no better than yours, Merry, ~ " he had said.

But they were. Merry saw this immediately. Before her were pictures drawn by other young people around the island, children she would never have suspected had talent at all, let alone this much. In her mind's eye, where before she had been so proud, now she saw her own work as rough, unschooled, too simple to be considered anything but the idle sketching of a girl with too much time on her hands.

She had stood for another moment, side by side with Ezra, studying. Then abruptly she turned away and began to walk, folding her own sheets of paper in half and putting them under her arm.

Ezra had caught her by a shoulder. " ~ Merry, Merry. Don't be so harsh on yourself. ~ " He had smiled down at her, offering encouragement. " ~ This is as good as going to school. We can both learn from this. ~ "

~ I've already learned. I haven't talent. ~

" ~ You do! It just hasn't ripened as quickly as others. ~ " Ezra had taken her arm then and steered her between people and booths to the out-of-doors.

They passed under the pillared porch of the grange hall and walked away, towards the road.

" ~ It takes time, you know, to develop skill, ~ " Ezra had counselled. " ~ When I was your age, Merry, I thought I was ready to go to sea. I knew the winds and the tides and I knew all about fishing. At least, I believed that I did. And maybe I did, too, but what I didn't have was the strength to use all this knowledge. ~ "

Merry had stood on the dusty ground that led away from the grange, her eyes locked on the toes of her shoes. Ezra put a hand under her chin and forced Merry to meet his eyes.

" ~ I needed to grow, Merry. I needed height and I needed heft. Until then, all I ever was in a boat was cargo. I couldn't pull my own load. Don't you see? ~ "

~ That has nothing to do with talent! ~

Ezra laughed. " ~ It does so. It's exactly the same thing. You're standing on the shore now, just as I did, looking at what seems to be so easy and simple to do. It isn't. That's all that's happened today. You learned. Drawing isn't simple. Fishing isn't simple. ~ " He winked. " ~ Life isn't simple. ~ "

~ I should have brought my stitchery, ~ Merry decided. ~ I'm very talented on the machine. Everyone says so. ~

Ezra shook his head, but kindly. " ~ Does sewing fill your soul, Merry? Does it make you happy? ~ "

~ It's not supposed to. It's something I do well, better than other girls. It's something the judges— ~

She couldn't finish her thought. Tears spilled and her shoulders began to shake.

Ezra reached out and with both arms brought his sister comfortingly into his body. He rocked her a moment before standing back. When Merry looked up into his face, she saw her own pain reflected in his brimming blue eyes.

" ~ Don't ever give up on yourself, Merry, ~ " her brother said seriously. " ~ Believe in yourself. Just think. If you weren't as bright as you are, if you weren't as sensible, Merry, you would have handed your work in only to be disappointed later. Think how fortunate you are to see clearly. Think how lucky you are you can take another year, or even two, before you know, deep down, that you really are as good as you want to be. ~ "

Dearest Ezra! How sympathetic he had been, how understanding. It was he, she had been certain, who had suggested that her father bestow upon her at Christmas her sketchbook, pens and inks. Oh, how she missed him now!

A shadow fell across her closed eyes. She opened them quickly, ready to leap off and away from whomever stood before her.

" ~ You cannot stay here, Merry. ~ "

Merry tried to make herself grow very small, to meld into the underbrush. Spaulding smiled at her efforts and shook his head. " ~ Your family knows, don't you see? ~ " he began. " ~ This morning Bailey got Eleanor to confess, to tell her where you were, and worse, from my point of view, why you were waiting here. ~ "

~ Oh, Spaulding, I'm so sorry. I never imagined that— ~

" ~ Nor did I. But that's water spilt. Now we have to hide you somewhere else. Your family will come looking for you this afternoon. They've looked for you everywhere. They'd have been here now but for chores and your father's old horse throwing a shoe. ~ "

Spaulding reached down for one of Merry's hands and pulled her to her feet. Even as he spoke, Spaulding felt ashamed of himself. " ~ You may not have to stay long, Merry. Mr. Fisher has sent men to look for the stranger at the post office. If they find him, if he really did kill Nickerson, you'd be entirely safe to return. ~ "

~ But suppose they don't! ~

" ~ Then you'll be no worse off than Gerry Daggett or Mr. West, will you? ~ "

Merry turned away from Spaulding Mayhew and focused

for a moment at the distant fairgrounds. Then she announced firmly, ~ They're men. ~

" ~ That doesn't mean they couldn't be guilty. ~ "

~ It means other men will give them the benefit of the doubt, before me. ~

" ~ Why did you hurl that stone so? ~ " Spaulding asked. " ~ It was all anyone talked of later. What made you do such a thing? ~ "

Merry shrugged. She had already given Spaulding her reason. It wasn't her fault if he couldn't understand.

Spaulding took a big breath. " ~ Look, Merry, we have to leave this place. People know about it. They'll come for you. Come along now, don't fight me. We have to find a safer haven. ~ "

Merry didn't budge. ~ What will you and Eleanor do now? ~

" ~ I don't know. We'll leave, that's for sure. If not tonight, then tomorrow. Or as soon as people think we've given up trying. ~ "

~ And am I to hide forever? ~

" ~ Merry, come on! Eleanor and I will get food to you. And clothing. We won't abandon you. But you must come now, away from the fair. ~ "

~ Spaulding! I have an idea! ~

But Spaulding's patience was growing shorter. He tugged at her.

Merry dug in her heels. ~ Stop! ~

Spaulding looked at Merry, doubtful. He glanced quickly at the fair beyond. Then wordlessly, he forced Merry to look back, too.

Franklin Fisher was strolling among the crowds. Behind him were Peter West and Jedediah Pease.

thirty-eight

Merry and Spaulding sat breathlessly just inside the double doors of the barn. After a moment, Merry got to her knees to crawl forward a pace to peer out, to see whether they were being followed. She saw no one.

She turned to see Spaulding huddled behind her, his head bowed, his hands over his ears.

Merry reached out.

At first Spaulding did not move. He wanted to share his misery with no one. How had he come to this strange pass, a murderer, a secret fugitive, trusting that justice alone would save others from what he himself deserved?

Now he hid a child, an ornery little girl, from the Law that she need never fear.

All he had meant to do was prove to Eleanor his devotion.

Merry shook Spaulding's shoulder gently. After a moment more, finally, he looked up, very slowly. ~ Do you want to hear my idea, Spaulding? ~

Spaulding shook his head.

~ It's a good one. I promise. I know you'll like it. ~

Spaulding sighed dramatically. " ~ What is it? ~ "

~ You and Eleanor must leave as planned. ~

Spaulding smiled as at a child. " ~ How do we do that, with her entire family set now against us? ~ "

~ They were before, ~ Merry reasoned. ~ Of course, they didn't know, but had they done, they would have been against you. ~

" ~ That's very comforting. ~ "

Merry smiled broadly. ~ Don't you see? They think they've stopped you! They think now you wouldn't dare carry Eleanor off as you planned. But you must! ~

Spaulding watched Merry's hands closely.

~ I doubt they'll even be watching now, ~ Merry continued. ~ As far as they know, your secret plan is no more. They would never imagine you would still carry it off, right on schedule, right under their noses! ~

" ~ Merry, they won't even allow Eleanor to— ~ "

But Merry was positive. ~ Yes, they will! I know my aunt. She'll think her good sense will have persuaded Eleanor from such an act. And I know Eleanor. She'll let her mother believe she has been persuaded. ~

Spaulding smiled, just a little. Eleanor was bright, he knew. And also stubborn. Maybe there was a little truth in what Merry was saying.

~ Aunt Elizabeth won't want her friends to know anything about this. So what will happen? The entire family will come to the fair today, just as they had planned. They daren't leave Eleanor alone, so they'll have to bring her. ~

" ~ And who will watch Eleanor every minute? ~ "

Merry sat back, content. ~ No one. It's just what I've done, you know. I've been under everyone's nose all along. And no one's found *me*! ~

Spaulding reached out and touched Merry's dress. " ~ They'd hardly recognize you if they did. ~ "

Merry brought a hand up to her hair and felt it. She knew Spaulding was joking, but she also knew she looked horrible—dirty, torn, scratched. She had a sudden fright. ~ Do I look so awful they won't let me board the steamer? ~

But Spaulding had stood and moved towards the doorway. Merry pulled herself up as well and went to stand beside him. Together they looked out silently at the distant fair. ~ You must go there. ~

Spaulding turned to look at Merry. ~ You must go there, ~ she repeated. ~ You're expected. Eleanor will need to see you there. ~

" ~ And then? ~ "

Merry beamed. ~ And then—you do exactly what you aimed to do all along! ~

Spaulding stood silently. Now it was Merry who grew impatient. Why did boys never see the simple truths of life? ~ Spaulding, if you love Eleanor—and I believe you do—you can do this. Perhaps you can steal away earlier. I don't know. But I do know you can do this if you want to. ~ She paused for a second. ~ I know that Eleanor would expect you to be as dashing and determined as this. You cannot disappoint her. ~

Merry needed Spaulding to believe her, and to believe in himself, desperately. If he would not continue with his plan, *her* escape route would be cut off.

Inwardly Spaulding was considering the power of what Merry was suggesting. More, he understood immediately that if he and Eleanor did not elope, *his* path to escape might be closed forever.

" ~ And what about you, Merry? ~ "

~ Me? Why, you know where I am. I am here, ready, waiting for you both. Anytime. ~

Spaulding studied her a moment somberly. He nodded. He turned and took a few steps away from the shelter of the barn. Then, with a speed that startled Merry, Spaulding began to run towards the fair at full tilt.

But he tripped!

Merry gasped.

Spaulding lay still upon the ground.

Merry started to move out of the shadows of the barn to help him. But she stopped. She saw his shoulders heaving.

Spaulding was lying on the ground sobbing.

Why? Merry asked herself. Why? she would have asked Spaulding had she been at his side.

But before she could make the decision that would expose her to Mr. Fisher and everyone else at the fair, Spaulding began to pull himself up to his knees slowly. His head was bent towards the earth. He must have been dazed, Merry decided.

For what seemed a moment of stopped time, Spaulding did not move.

Merry could not understand.

At last, with what seemed a gigantic effort, Spaulding rose. Without a look back at Merry, but with just the slightest wave of his hand, he began again to run towards the fair.

thirty-nine

Alone once more, Merry turned away from the open barn doors and stepped back into the comforting, dark smells of animals, equipment, and feed.

She walked thoughtfully along the center aisle, between pens and stalls. What had she to do between now and whenever Spaulding arrived with Eleanor?

Before she could answer herself, she jumped back, startled. An aged horse with hardly any teeth left had stuck out its head in front of her. She hadn't even known there were animals left in the barn. Usually all were herded out to feed or exercise.

She put up her hand and stroked the horse's nose gently. Poor thing. No more happy runs for you.

Her hand dropped quickly. How many happy runs would there be for *her*?

Merry pushed the thought away.

She turned and started back towards the barn doors. The one thing she could do, she decided, was try to make herself more presentable. Of course it would be night when she arrived in Vineyard Haven with Eleanor and Spaulding; it would be dawn when they boarded the ferry. But there would be lights in town, at dockside and perhaps even on deck. Three young people sailing the Sound might not be unusual, but two with a third bedraggled, wretched-looking tag-along would be.

There was a trough not more than thirty feet away from where she stood. Its water might not be clean enough to drink, but it would be to wash. Dare she?

Merry felt she had no choice. Peeking out to look one way and then the other, and seeing no human form, she dashed forwards. She plunged her hands into the cool water and swiped at her face and her arms. Without thinking she brought up the hem of her skirt to use as a towel.

She ran back towards the barn and stood still dripping in its doorway, unaware that the dirt from her dress had been splashed across her nose and cheeks.

She looked at the sky. There was still time to wait. Before long, the animals that belonged to the farm would return to be milked or curried or simply turned in and fed. She needed a place to hide, in case Eleanor and Spaulding were delayed. After all she had done, she certainly didn't want to be accidentally discovered by a farmer striding into what he thought was an empty barn.

Merry squinted back into the barn, rejecting one corner and then another. She looked upwards, into the loft. But if she were to stay there, there was no guarantee the farmer might not climb the ladder as well, in order to throw down hay for his herd.

After a few moments, Merry decided that the best she could hope for was to remain unnoticed in a dark corner where bridles and saddlery hung. There was a huge beam there around which she could duck, too, if she needed.

If, she thought. If. If Spaulding arrived with Eleanor, if they weren't seen running towards Vineyard Haven, if they could get aboard the steamer, if—if Spaulding had money enough for three fares.

What would *Merry* do about money? The idea that she was no longer to remain on the island was still so foreign to her that she had seldom thought about needing any. But she knew, from her time in Hartford, that in the rest of the world it was necessary.

Oh, what could she do now, so late, so close to sailing away?

Despite every good intention, Merry's eyes filled. She did not want to leave the island. She had never even imagined living somewhere else. She could not imagine what skill she might have to trade for food or shelter. And she had certainly never thought about being separated from her family forever.

forty

Although there was still a blush of daylight, Merry felt exhausted. And she was beginning to feel a chill.

For fear of being taken unawares, she had paced the barn a thousand times, walking its central aisle, crossing from stall to stall, standing at the doorway looking out over the fields. While she was used to walking—to school, to the store on errands for Molly, to the shore to draw or to trade for blue crabs—her legs ached all the way down to her ankles. It seemed to her that she had been standing or running for four days without rest.

To keep herself alert, Merry peeked around one of the barn doors and looked over at the fair. Candles and lamps were beginning to wink back at her. Soon, she knew, people would move indoors, fiddlers would tune their instruments, dancing would begin.

She wondered whether Eleanor would dance that night.

Daylight was fading. Merry stared for a moment at the

fair, remembering how much she would usually have enjoyed being there, looking at the displays, sampling food, admiring livestock.

Ever wary, she looked over her shoulder to see whether whoever owned this farm was yet returning. She saw no one. She turned her gaze back towards the fair.

Suddenly, in the twilight, she saw a thin figure running directly at her.

She ducked back inside the barn and whirled, looking for her corner. She could only hope that with light disappearing out-of-doors, the interior of the barn would be even darker. She scooted around the gigantic beam she had earlier found and held her breath.

Simon Mayhew ran right into the barn.

He stood for a moment without moving, panting. He looked one way and then another. Then he smiled and walked directly towards Merry's corner.

~ What are you doing here? ~ Merry demanded. ~ How did you find me? ~

Simon took several big breaths to calm himself. " ~ Spaulding told me. ~ "

~ Spaulding! ~

Simon nodded.

~ But— ~

Simon put out his hand to stop her. " ~ He sent me with these, ~ " Simon offered, holding out two still warm buns from the fair.

Merry stared at them for a second before taking them and beginning to nibble at one hungrily. Simon touched her shoulder. " ~ Tell me again what the man at the post office looked like. ~ "

Merry swallowed dryly. ~ I don't know what he looked like. I told you. What light there was was behind me. It shone on his clothes, not his face. I noticed only his clothes. ~

Simon nodded, remembering. " ~ His vest. What colors had it? ~ "

Merry shrugged. ~ Bright ones. Colors we don't see here on the island. Fancy. ~

Simon smiled. " ~ I think he's at the fair. ~ "

Merry swallowed more soft bun.

" ~ He's right out there, for anyone to see! ~ " Simon went on excitedly. " ~ Only Mr. Fisher hasn't seen him. I bet he's walked by this man a hundred times and hasn't tumbled! ~ "

Merry wiped her hands on her skirt. " ~ Where have you been? ~ " Simon now asked, pretending to be angry. " ~ How could you run away from me, your friend, like that? Where did you go? How did you spend the night? ~ "

~ Why doesn't Mr. Fisher see the man? ~

Simon shrugged. " ~ I guess no one paid as much attention to him last Saturday night as you did. I mean, other people remember a stranger, but no one else seemed to have noticed his vest. ~ "

~ You must tell Mr. Fisher that. ~

Simon looked startled. " ~ But, Merry, I— ~ "

~ You must point the man out! It's your duty! ~

" ~ But it wasn't I who saw him. It was you! Everyone knows where I was that night. You're the one who was afoot then, not me. You saw him. ~ "

Merry thought about this.

" ~ Merry, you must come to the fair. *You* must tell Mr. Fisher. ~ "

Walking onto the fairgrounds would be like lifting another fatal stone, Merry thought to herself.

Fleetingly she wished Eleanor and Spaulding had arrived

instead of Simon. Then she could be far away and never have to make this kind of decision.

But if the man had killed Ned Nickerson?

It was her only hope.

But suppose it wasn't the same man?

How would she know if she didn't . . . ?

Merry reached out for Simon's hand and stepped into the twilight.

forty-one

" ~ It's a good thing I came for you, ~ " Simon said, pointing back as they walked.

Merry looked towards the barn. A tall man, wearing boots, britches and a heavy jacket, was trailing his herd of cattle into it.

Merry ran a few paces until she was safely out of sight of the barn. She didn't slow until she was once more in the cover of the thin line of trees that separated the fairgrounds from the farm she had borrowed for the day.

" ~ There! ~ " Simon pointed. " ~ Look there! ~ "

Merry followed Simon's finger. She studied the fairgrounds through the trees. She turned to Simon and shrugged.

" ~ There, there! ~ " he insisted, pointing again. " ~ Right in front of those canvas walls. ~ "

Merry looked again. She saw a small tentlike structure but without a roof: four large pieces of canvas held upright by long poles, with a door cut in one canvas flap, standing about eight feet high. Hand-painted above this makeshift entryway was a sign: DIME MUSEUM, SEE UNTOLD WONDERS!

Standing in front of this enticement was a fairly stout man, not too tall, wearing a rounded hat. ~ Him? ~ Merry asked Simon.

Simon nodded eagerly. " ~ You can't really see him in this light, from this distance, ~ " he told her. " ~ But when you get up close, you can see he's wearing the exact same weskit you told me about! ~ "

Simon would have talked on a bit, about how he had run across this man, what was in his tent. But suddenly Merry was pushed against him roughly.

Pickup, holding onto Merry's skirt, looking excitedly up into her face, had a lot of questions that needed to be answered *now*. "Where have you been? Where did you go last night? Did you eat anything? Weren't you scared?"

Merry pulled away from her brother. ~ What are you saying? ~

Pickup repeated all his questions, this time more carefully. But Merry only shook her head stubbornly. ~ How did you find me? ~ she asked suspiciously.

" ~ Eleanor told us where you'd be, ~ " Pickup replied. " ~ She told us you'd be here, waiting for the fair to close. ~ " Then he smiled like a conspirator. " ~ And she told us where she and Spaulding Mayhew were going. And that you were going with them! ~ "

Merry ignored all this. ~ Where's Papa? ~

" ~ Bringing Ma and Bailey across the fair. Look. See them? ~ "

Merry turned to see—not only her family but Franklin Fisher, Peter West, Jedediah Pease.

Every ounce of Merry's remaining strength seemed to evaporate into the October air. Not meaning to, perhaps not even noticing that she did so, she leaned heavily against Simon.

Simon steadied himself. " ~ Are you all right? ~ "

~ Oh Simon, maybe I should just surrender. I'm so tired. ~

" ~ You cannot! You just cannot. The man you saw, the man other people saw, is right over there! I promise you! ~ "

"Where? Who?" whispered Pickup.

But before he could be answered, Merry sat down hard on the ground. She hung her head, shaking it back and forth.

Simon knelt quickly beside her.

~ You go, Simon. I haven't the heart. Suppose that is the man I saw. And then suppose he had nothing to do with killing Ned Nickerson. What hope would I have? ~

" ~ The same hope Peter West and Gerry Daggett have! The same even as Henny Chapell. ~ "

Merry couldn't think how this might aid her cause. ~Why shouldn't there be four trials? ~ she asked.

" ~ Merry, there is no clear evidence against any of you. All Mr. Fisher knows is that you weren't at home when Nickerson was killed, and that each of you is strong enough to have killed him. There are no known reasons for doing so. ~ " He paused, a scowl crossing his features. " ~ Unless on South Beach something happened, something really serious. ~ "

Merry shook her head and straightened where she sat. She looked across the field towards the fair.

Pickup was running like a rabbit towards her family. And towards Mr. Fisher!

forty-two

Forgetting how tired she was, Merry leapt to her feet. Simon did the same. Even as Pickup ran, his arm above his head, shouting to get the quick attention of his family, Merry was backing away towards the shadows of the trees.

Simon read her mind. He reached out for her hand and grasped it, holding it tightly.

Merry looked at her friend, her eyes begging him to release her. Simon was firm. He took a step towards the fairgrounds.

Merry was shaking her head as Simon pulled harder, but she allowed him his way.

Together they emerged from the tree line. At the fair, Benjamin had taken a step away from his family. He looked across the field, through the sheds, towards where Merry and Simon were approaching. Suddenly Bailey ran past him.

" ~ Oh, Merry! ~ " Bailey said breathlessly, stepping back from her embrace of her sister. " ~ How could you disappear like that? We've all been so worried! Oh, how glad I am to see you safe! ~ "

Merry only smiled thinly. She was too tired to argue that she might not be safe at all, or even ever again.

Bailey put her arm over Merry's shoulder and together, followed by Simon, they continued back to the fairgrounds, past the sheds, past the exhibition ring. Past a number of townspeople who stared and pointed.

Molly Skiffe embraced her daughter, controlling her urge to let Merry know just how angry she was. Relieved to be sure, but angry, too, to have been so frightened for her daughter overnight. She could see that most of the fight had gone out of her younger daughter. Her own love for her was too great to add scolding to Merry's load.

Benjamin Skiffe was holding Merry tightly when Mr. Fisher's hand landed upon his shoulder. Before Merry's father could face the man or even begin to think what to say that would continue to protect her, Merry had stepped out of his arms and was looking directly up into Mr. Fisher's somber face. ~ That is the man I saw, ~ Merry announced.

She pointed towards the Dime Museum, some fifty feet away, as Simon spoke on Merry's behalf.

Mr. Fisher followed Merry's finger. "Is she certain?" he asked of the entire family.

" ~ Yes, she is, ~ " Simon Mayhew answered quickly. " ~ He's from off-island. Just ask him. He's probably the killer! ~ "

Peter West smiled gently at Simon's certainty.

Pickup, not waiting to hear Simon's accusation, had dashed away from his family's reunion to stand eagerly at the stout man's elbow. "What's in there?" he asked.

The man turned to look down at Pickup. He had a ruddy face with creases in it from hearty eating and drinking. He pushed back the hat on his head and half-knelt towards Pickup, his voice cheerful and amused.

"What's in here?" he asked in return. "Why, just some of the Seven Wonders of the World, that's what. Just what every young lad like yourself should see!"

"What do you mean? What wonders?"

166

The man swept his arm in front of his tent. "Why, I've got a man in there who has skin like a snake's!"

Pickup gasped. "No!"

The man nodded. "I do. And more than that, I've got the largest woman in the northeast, so big—why she's as big as any cow you can think of, guernsey or Jersey like you have here. Bigger even than the poor old Holsteins who got wiped out in the plague of 'sixty-nine!"

Pickup's eyes were round as pewter plates.

"This is educational, my boy," the man went on happily. "Your whole family would benefit from seeing what's behind these walls. I've got a man in there who looks exactly like a chicken! You've never seen anything like it, I daresay. Nor your family, either. You should *rush* to get your family, my boy, before the fair closes and you lose your last and only chance to see these amazing sights."

Convinced that in three minutes he would have half-a-dozen new customers for his museum, the man drew himself up to his full height, which wasn't very tall, and swung out his arms expansively. "The whole township should take advantage of this final offer!"

The man beamed down at Pickup before turning his eyes to the fairground field behind him. Then suddenly, he paled and drew back towards the tent. His very nightmares had taken shape, had come to life, and were marching directly at him!

Mr. Fisher, Mr. West, and the very tall, dark and dour Jedediah Pease were not more than half a dozen paces from him. Just behind them was another huge man, Benjamin Skiffe, and a growing crowd of onlookers, women and children.

His dreams were real! He began to perspire, even though the late-afternoon air was now chill. Faintly he heard fiddles being tuned in the hall.

The group halted before the tent. Mr. Fisher turned to Merry. "Is this the man you saw Saturday night last?"

Merry did not need this question translated. She nodded her head. ~ I did not see his face. I saw his vest. ~

"May we learn your name?" Mr. Fisher asked of the trembling man.

"Smith!" The answer had come unbidden.

"Smith," Mr. Fisher echoed, not smiling.

"Patrick O'Connor . . . Smith." A little detail like that couldn't hurt. "From Portland. South Portland, in truth."

"Well, Mr. Smith, how came you to this island?"

"By boat, sir. By boat," the man named "Smith" answered. Perhaps he was wrong. How could he know? What *should* he say?

Mr. Fisher nodded slowly. "Would that have been Saturday last, sir?"

"Saturday morning," Smith replied quickly, wanting despite his fear to seem to be helpful.

"At what landfall?" Mr. Fisher asked.

Merry studied the round little fellow. He seemed quite normal. Though his figure appeared soft and used to a different sort of living than what Martha's Vineyard provided, he also looked quite strong. He had crinkles and dimples all over his face, from laughing, from looking into the sun.

"At Menemsha," Mr. Smith answered. "Menemsha, yes. I should say at noon, or shortly thereafter. Yes, it must have been, noon."

"How came you to the fair, sir? By horse or by foot?"

"Afoot, sir," Smith was quick to say. "I was led by people with whom I spoke as I debarked to expect my destination lay not far away. So, by foot."

Pickup noticed sudden movements behind the canvas. There

were people behind those soft walls, listening! The chicken man!

"Your destination, sir," Mr. Fisher continued. "Was it an hotel? Were you to stay with friends?"

"Yes!" Mr. Smith nearly cried. "Friends. I was to stay with friends!" Oh, he knew now. Oh, he knew! "Sir, I am a kind man, a man of good intent, with children of my own."

Mr. Fisher nodded, but seemed not impressed. "And your friends there, behind those walls, did they travel with you?"

Mr. Smith paled even more, his face the color of tallow.

Before he could think what to reply, Jedediah Pease stepped close to him. He scowled down at the shorter man and raised his hands. ~ Did you kill Nickerson? ~

But Pease's question was incomprehensible to Smith, who jumped back in terror against the canvas behind him, cowering, raising his own arms above his head and wincing, ducking, peering out in horror. "Don't strike me!" he cried. "Don't strike!"

Ben Skiffe and Peter West had taken companionable steps forward with Jedediah Pease. The tiny fellow looked up into a dark wall. Mr. Fisher took another step forward, as well.

"Where were you Saturday night last, sir? Did you speak with anyone? Did you see anyone along the road? What direction did you travel? Did you stop?"

Merry felt sorry for the little man. He was so frightened. She could hardly imagine someone like this killing Mr. Nickerson. She found suddenly she didn't even want to believe that he had.

"I was lost!" shouted Mr. Smith. "Yes, lost, I was lost! It was growing dark, and my destination . . . I . . . I was lost."

"Did you ask directions of anyone?" Mr. Fisher asked.

Mr. Smith lowered his arms. But within seconds they were up and flying again.

"If you please, sir, with your permission, a little patience, please, sir. Yes, 'tis true, lost I was. It was dark and I knew nothing of my surroundings. I came to a building in which there was candlelight. It appeared welcoming to me, so I stopped.

"An innocent abroad is what I was," Mr. Smith said, beginning to warm a bit to the picture he drew. "A poor wanderer, lost on a distant isle, in a far clime. I needed assistance, of course I did. And so I sought it.

"But what I received in return for my polite inquiry were threats, sir. I met within that building a dozen men, forbidding all, who, when I asked for comfort, strode towards me, hands waving in the air, horrible sounds issuing from their mouths. I was in terror for my life, sir, absolutely! My very life was on the threshold of extinction, I assure you!"

Bailey, standing at Merry's side and between her and Mr. Fisher, translated as quickly as she could the tale the stranger spun. But Merry was not paying attention. There was something unknown—no, something known but dimly—that was trying to come to the surface of her memory.

"Not withstanding, sir," Mr. Smith hurried on, "nothing withstanding, I introduced myself and offered my card—" and here Smith dug into a pocket of his vest and pulled out a card to hand to Mr. Fisher.

Mr. Fisher looked down at the piece of heavy embossed paper. "Well, Mr. . . . Jones, what is it that happened?"

"What happened?! I'll tell you exactly what happened! Courteous though I was, a traveller in a strange land needing nothing but a few words of guidance, or perhaps a cup of something to see me on my way, what did I get in return, sir? I'll tell you what I got, sir, I got the threat of extinction! Those men were out to murder me!

"What was a man to do, I ask you, sir, what would any God-fearing citizen have done in the face of such hostility? He would have fled, sir, just as I did. Out into the black night, his legs carrying him as fast as they could away to safety in some dank hidey-hole. With neither shelter nor friend, a man like myself did what he would have to. Flee for the sake of his poor wife and children, sir! Who hoped, nay expected, when they saw him off the day before that he would soon return to them safe and happy, a bit heavier of pocket for the good of them all!"

Bailey's hands had been frantically repeating all this to Merry in the twilight, but Merry was fascinated by this man. He seemed like a creature from another civilization, a wildly colored round little bird that was terrified, lost and frightened by any sudden shadow.

Mr. Fisher was growing impatient. He cut off Mr. Jones's recitation with his hand slicing through the air between them. "Tell me, sir, did you meet anyone else on the road? As you fled? Did you meet anyone else?"

Mr. Smith-and-Jones staggered at the question.

"Come, sir. The truth. Did you spend the remainder of that night alone?"

Mr. Jones's eyes began to fill, even as he opened his round little mouth to speak. But before he could say a word, Mr. Fisher hurled a javelin at his heart. "A man was murdered, Mr. Jones, that very night, not far from where you asked for assistance. A man was killed. What do you know of that, sir?"

"Killed?" Mr. Jones asked in a whisper. "Killed? No, not killed. Surely not killed!"

Mr. Fisher stood motionlessly, his arms crossing his chest, waiting.

Mr. Jones clasped his hands together, lacing and unlacing his fingers. "Not killed, sir," he said finally, in a very low voice. "That was not the intent, sir. No, sir, that was not the intent."

"What was the intent?" Mr. Fisher asked shortly.

"Why, safety, sir. Safety, my very own life and limb. I had fled from that miserable band of cutthroats, men who for no reason on God's earth decided I must die. I ran, sir, I admit that. It wasn't brave, but run I did.

"In total darkness, all alone and half-witted I fled for my life. And as I ran along the path, I heard hoofbeats behind me. I looked over my shoulder and saw a horseman gaining on me. He rode an enormous steed, sir, the biggest I had ever seen, and as he bore down on me I had only one thought, to escape, to live again to see my poor family.

"I leapt a wall, sir. I leapt a wall and breathless stood waiting, crouched down behind the stones, knowing that at any minute the horse would draw up and its master smite me a blow from which I would never recover.

"I grasped at what was at hand, sir, at whatever my fingers could find in the blackness to save me. I found a loose stone, sir, atop the wall. I didn't think about it, sir. I didn't. My fingers, my hand, my arm did all my thinking for me. A man—perhaps the very angel of death—was riding at me like a cyclone, silent but vengeful, though I knew not of what deed. I had to protect myself, sir. It was him or me, anyone could see that, anyone!"

Mr. Jones hardly took a breath.

"I wasn't thinking, sir, I was acting. I may not seem like a man of grand gesture or noble deed, but I am a man, sir, for all that. I crouched there, waiting in terror, but determined to live. When the horse came even with me, when it had run a pace beyond, I stepped out and hurled the stone in my hand.

"In the terrifying blackness that surrounded me, I could not see, I could not say even now, that the stone struck its target. But the steed and its rider continued on into the darkness ahead of me. Not waiting to discover whether I was in fact free of the shadow of death, I turned and fled across the fields, sir, across streams and fields, through forest and glade, not lighthearted, mind you. Not free of fear. But safe, sir, safe!"

Four tall men took another step towards Mr. Jones.

Not expecting to be answered, nor even wanting a reply, Bailey turned to her sister. " ~ It's hard, isn't it, ~ " she said, " ~ understanding something when you are so frightened. ~ "

But Merry seemed in a trance. Suddenly she nodded, as though what she had sought in her memory had come clear, and she stepped away from Bailey and towards Mr. Jones.

She pushed her way past Mr. Fisher, Peter West, her father and Jedediah Pease. ~ Stop! ~ Merry demanded, looking quickly over her shoulder at her father.

Facing the four men, she stood planted directly in front of Mr. Jones who seemed to grow smaller and more helpless by the second, so certain was he of rough justice.

~ Stop, ~ Merry insisted again. ~ This is not the man who killed Mr. Nickerson! ~

"What does she say?" asked Mr. Jones from behind her, trembling even more at what he could not grasp.

Bailey moved a bit forward to translate now for both Mr. Fisher and Mr. Smith/Jones.

" ~ How are you so certain, Merry? ~ " Peter West inquired. " ~ From the man's own mouth we hear that— ~ "

Merry shook her head, cutting Mr. West off. ~ I was on the road that night, ~ she announced. ~ I was nearby. I had left the post office, as you all know. I was on my way home. ~

~ Merry, what— ~

But even Merry's father was forced to wait. ~ On my way, I saw a chewink, a hurt little bird on my path. I had in mind rescuing him, bringing him home to be cared for and nursed. Just as I picked him up, he was startled and fell to the ground. What scared him wasn't me, Papa. It was a horse, a big horse, Mr. Nickerson's horse! On the road beside me, I saw Mr. Nickerson's horse crashing towards Indian Hill. ~

"Please, gentlemen, I beg you! Am I to be accused and not even aware of the words that seek so to slay me?"

"Silence!" Mr. Fisher cautioned severely. "Let the girl finish."

Mr. Jones hung his head. He rocked a little from one foot to the other, his eyes clenched tightly against the unknown.

~ To be fair, ~ Merry added thoughtfully, ~ all I can say with certainty is that the horse I saw in the shadows might have been Mr. Nickerson's. But there is no other on the island I know of such great size and power, so I believe it must have been his. ~

Merry took a big breath. ~ When that horse had passed, I ran after the bird once more. Again I nearly had him in my hands when something new scared the wee thing and it darted away from me forever, into the underbrush and out of sight. What could have startled it so? Why, it must have been a second horse, a smaller horse, speeding past us both, although it was a horse I did not turn to see. ~

"You mean you think Mr. Nickerson was being chased?" asked Mr. Fisher then.

Merry looked at Bailey. ~ I don't know whether he was being set upon, ~ Merry admitted honestly. ~ I only believe that he was being followed close by. ~

"But is it not common of a Saturday night for people to be abroad?" asked Mr. Fisher thoughtfully.

Merry nodded reasonably. ~ But at night, who but a soul in peril would race heedlessly in such thin moonlight? ~ She turned to look at Mr. Jones who, still uncomprehending, stared back at her, quivering. ~ This poor man has told us he was afoot that night. Someone, I know not his name, someone else rode in the darkness. That someone, sir, must be the man you seek. ~

" ~ And besides, ~ " Simon Mayhew stepped forward to say, " ~ no man quickly grasps a stone when a boulder is what he needs! ~ "

No one spoke, all thoughtful, for a moment. Then Simon announced excitedly, " ~ Mr. Nickerson's killer is still at large! ~ "

Mr. Fisher looked from Simon to Merry and back again at Simon before lowering his gaze. He chose to say nothing. The boy was right.

forty-three

A series of jolts caused by ruts beneath the Skiffe trap woke Merry. She had been riding between her parents, wrapped in one of her mother's shawls, her head on Molly's shoulder, sleeping.

Benjamin had turned Back-'n'-Fill south, from the Edgartown-Tisbury road, onto the path that led to his farm. Back-'n'-Fill's pace increased and Ben held his reins more tightly and shorter. It would not do to let a horse bolt for home, as they were often wont to do.

Merry's parents had not questioned her closely about her trek cross country, about whom she had met, what she had thought to be doing, fleeing from the Law. Their daughter was spent. Her strength seemed feeble, her shoulders collapsed forward, not in shame but in exhaustion. There would be time enough to talk with her.

Nor had they spoken, even between themselves, of a joke on a poor stranger gone sour.

Merry sat up, pulling away from Molly's arm. She looked first at the moon which seemed to be grinning down at her alone, as relieved as she was. Then she saw where the trap was, what trees and shrubs it passed in the light from above, and she put her hand on Benjamin's. He turned to look at her.

~ Stop, please stop. ~

Benjamin wrapped Back-'n'-Fill's reins tightly around the armrest at his side. ~ But Merry, dear, we are nearly home. ~

Merry nodded. ~ I know, Pa. I know. But please, please stop. ~

~ Oh, of course. I understand. ~ He reached for the reins.

Merry could not help smiling. ~ No, Pa, it's not that. Truly. I just want to walk, alone. I need to walk home. ~

Ben looked beyond his daughter at his wife. After a second, Molly nodded understandingly.

The trap slowed enough for Merry to lean over her mother and to jump to the ground. In the back, Pickup lay in Bailey's arms, sound asleep.

Merry looked up at her mother. ~ I shan't be long, Ma. ~

" ~ It's chill, dear. Don't dawdle. ~ "

~ No, I won't. ~

After a second, Benjamin urged Back-'n'-Fill forward again and Merry was soon part of the shadows that fell across the road.

She stood motionlessly a moment in the center of the path, watching her father's trap disappear in the distance and dark. Then she wrapped her mother's shawl more tightly about her shoulders and walked at a slow and deliberate pace. She looked again at the moon and smiled rather sadly.

Poor Mr. Jones, she thought. Frightened out of his wits, not knowing that the way Ned Nickerson bore down on him was the way Ned Nickerson bore down on anyone in his way. Mr. Nickerson might not even have been able to see Mr. Jones in the road ahead that terrible night.

It was just as Bailey had said.

And when it had been made clear that Mr. Jones—not really a coward, Merry decided—was not the culprit the island sought, Bailey and she had turned away from the Dime Museum, its unseen treasures totally ignored.

In a moment, her family had turned to follow. Even Pickup walked away from the tent, somehow knowing that to be too curious, to want to stop longer at the fair to see the wonders of which Mr. Jones had spoken so proudly, would be disallowed. Merry felt badly for her brother. Tomorrow, when he awoke, Pickup would remember that he had been to the fair, all right, but that he had experienced almost nothing of its color and gaiety, its sights and smells. And he would blame her.

Merry shook off her momentary sadness. She looked at the sides of the path, happy to see trees she knew, bushes from whose branches she had picked hot summer treats. She had clambered silently through the forests and pastures of the island so happily for all the years of her life that she could not—did not have to now!—ever think of leaving. This was her home. This was where she belonged, where she would live out whatever years the Lord gave her.

That some unknown person still roamed these same forests and fields with blood on his hands disturbed her but she would have to put her trust and faith in Mr. Fisher, and in time.

She wondered now whether Eleanor and Spaulding had eloped amid the excitement of finding Mr. Jones. She had seen neither at the fairgrounds. Perhaps they had fled earlier than was planned, were even now asleep in someone's extra room before leaping aboard the early-morning steamer.

She was hugely relieved not to be at sea, facing a world about which she knew a little but in which she did not yet feel at home. Idly, she wondered whether she ever would.

She asked herself whether Eleanor herself would be happy across the Sound.

Eleanor was more of a mystery to Merry than she had been before. Before Spaulding, anyway, Merry added to herself. Eleanor had such an adventurous spirit, yet she seemed willing to forget her daring in favor of Spaulding's. Merry wondered whether Eleanor's behavior, too, was altered so entirely when she was with him. One thing Merry did know: whenever Eleanor spoke of Spaulding, she did so with a strange, bemused smile upon her lips, her eyes aglow as though by candlelight.

Merry had watched grown women, which Eleanor nearly was, women whom she knew to be smarter and more capable than their husbands. Yet each seemed always to sit behind, stand apart, to allow her husband to think he and he alone knew what was best for her and even their children.

Would she have to do this, too, when a husband appeared for her?

She wondered suddenly, even as she put the question to herself, whether women pretended all the time. Or at least when their husbands were about.

If so, Merry decided, stooping beneath an overhanging bough of a pine, life would be very difficult, indeed. She would watch to see what Bailey did.

She thought again of the cowering figure of Mr. Jones, the butt of an unwitting but common enough joke. And she smiled to recall the joke Bailey, Simon and she herself had played on another of Simon's cousins, Philip Mayhew, visiting the island from Plymouth.

On his arrival, Simon's cousin had caught sight of Bailey

near dockside in Menemsha and had been, so Simon told Merry, immediately "smitten." He implored his young cousin to affect an introduction to the lovely girl. Simon had complied, bringing Philip to the Skiffe home late one afternoon for tea.

Without once even discussing what they would do, how they would confound the rather bookish young gentleman, all three had pretended that Bailey herself could hear nothing. Philip was so enamored of Bailey, however, that this mattered nothing to him.

He paid her flowery compliments, "translated" by Simon, and Bailey mutely returned his attentions, answering his questions and leading him on, all in sign.

When it came time to depart, and tea had been served, Bailey stood from her chair and offered Philip Mayhew her hand in parting. She smiled affectionately at him. "Thank you for coming to see me," she said easily and clearly. "You have given me great pleasure."

The look on Philip Mayhew's face—of astonishment, of surprise, of embarrassment that he had been taken in so easily—threw his three attendants into gales of laughter, both loud and silent.

Merry smiled a moment to remember the scene but then she sobered. That had been done by daylight. That was a joke played fairly and where no dangerous misunderstanding could occur. But Mr. Jones had suffered for days before being given his reprieve. Seeing the relief on his face, watching Mr. Jones straighten and try to pull himself and his small dignity from around his feet, did not quite square all accounts.

Thinking a moment more, Merry decided that in time Mr. Jones would recover his good humor, just as she now felt herself doing. For she was walking freely across her own land, amid her own rock-strewn fields and dark forests, no longer fleeing from the eyes and arms of her neighbors.

Tomorrow, in the sunlight, her notebook and pens in her hands, she would amble through a neighbor's field, searching for the chokecherry tree that all summer she had been meaning to draw.

Acknowledgments

For assistance, encouragement, patience and enthusiasm beyond what might be reasonably expected of the kindest of people:

Jody Taylor Barasch, M.Ed.D., Education of the Deaf, Boston University; Winston P. Foote; Jane Ward, John Koza, and William La Moy of the Phillips Library of the Peabody–Essex Museum, Salem, Massachusetts; "Chronicle," produced by WCVB-TV, Boston, Massachusetts.

At the American School for the Deaf, West Hartford, Connecticut: Winfield McChord, Jr., executive director; Michelle Keifer; Mary McGleoin.

On Martha's Vineyard: Catherine Thompson and Kristin Maloney of the Chilmark Public Library; Eulalie Regan of *The Vineyard Gazette*; Susan Whiting, Joan Poole Nash, and, most especially, for her patience, research, and general good spirits, Harriette Poole Otteson.

anonymous. *The Country Picture Book for Boys and Girls*, primer and verse. New York: James G. Gregory, Publisher, 1862.

anonymous. *The Cottage City, or The Season at Martha's Vineyard*. Lawrence, Mass.: Merrill & Crocker Printers, 1879.

Baker, George Pierce. *Formation of the New England Railroad Systems*. Cambridge, Mass.: Harvard University Press, 1937.

Banks, Charles Edward, M.D. *History of Martha's Vineyard*. 3 vols. Edgartown, Mass.: Dukes County Historical Society, 1911 (reissued in 1966).

"Chilmark Master Plan," including the Open Space Plan prepared by the Joint Venture of the Chilmark Planning Board, the Chilmark Conservation Commission, Martha's Vineyard Commission, April 1985.

Close, F. Perry. *History of Hartford Streets*. Hartford: Connecticut Historical Society, 1969.

Davenport, Millia. *The Book of Costume*. New York: Crown Publishers, 1948.

Dunlap, Tom. "Where Silence Reigns." *Martha's Vineyard* magazine, May/June 1991.

Foster, Birket. illus. by. *Country Life*, selected poetry for children by Herrick, Smollet, Coleridge, Walton et al. New York and London: George Routledge & Sons, 1873.

Garrett, Elisabeth Donaghy. *At Home: the American Family 1750–1870*. New York: Harry N. Abrams, 1990.

Geer, Elihu. Canvassed and compiled by *Hartford City Directory*. Hartford Steam Printing Co., No. 42, July 1879.

Gorsline, Douglas. *What People Wore*. New York: Bonanza Books, 1952.

Groce, Nora Ellen. *Everyone Here Spoke Sign Language, Hereditary Deafness on Martha's Vineyard*. Cambridge, Mass. and London: Harvard University Press, 1985.

Hale, Anna. *Moraine to Marsh*. Vineyard Haven, Mass.: Watership Gardens, 1988.

Hartford Board of Trade, issued by the. *Hartford, Connecticut 1889, as a Manufacturing, Business and Commercial Center*. The Case, Lockwood, Brainard Co., printers.

Hough, Henry Beetle. *Martha's Vineyard, Summer Resort 1835–1935*. Rutland, Vt.: Tuttle Publishing Co., 1936.

Johnson, Cuthbert W. *The Farmer's Encyclopaedia*, adapted for the United States by Gouverneur Emerson. Philadelphia: Carey and Hart, 1844.

Kirkland, Edward Chase. *Men, Cities and Transportation, A Study in New England's History, 1820–1900*. Cambridge, Mass.: Harvard University Press, 1948.

Mader, Sylvia S. *Martha's Vineyard Nature Guide*. Edgartown, Mass.: Mader Enterprises.

Mitchell, Edwin Valentine. *Horse and Buggy Age in New England*. New York: Coward–McCann Publishers, 1937.

Norton, Henry Franklin. *Martha's Vineyard, Histories, Legends, Stories*. Hartford: Norton & Pyne Publishers, 1923.

Partridge, Bellamy. *As We Were: Family Life in America 1850–1900*. New York/London: McGraw–Hill/Whittlesey House, 1946.

Rawson, Marion. *Forever the Farm*. New York: E. P. Dutton and Co., Inc., 1939.

Rittenhouse, Jack D. *American Horse-Drawn Vehicles*. Los Angeles: Dillon Litograph Company for J. D. Rittenhouse, Publisher, 1948.

Russell, Howard S. *A Long, Deep Furrow: Three Centuries of Farming in New England*. Hanover, NH: University Press of New England, 1976.

Scott, Jonathan Fletcher. *The Early Colonial Houses of Martha's Vineyard*. 2 vols., Ph.D. thesis, University of Minnesota, September 1985.

Straus, Ralph. *Carriages and Coaches*. Philadelphia: J. B. Lippincott Co., 1912.

Turnbull, J. Hammond, ed. *The Memorial History of Hartford County*. 3 vols. Boston: Edward L. Osgood, publisher, 1986.

Van Cleve, John Vickrey, and Barry A. Crouch. *A Place of Their Own*. Washington, DC: Gallaudet University Press, 1989.

Williams–Mitchell, Christobel. *Dressed for the Job*. Poole, Dorset: Blandsford Press, 1982.